Never
"Just Natalie"

We were ushered into Michelle's living room. Noel was there. Was his smile especially for me, or was it just a smile left over from looking at Michelle? Then I noticed a man and a woman who were probably his parents.

"This is the little girl I was telling you about," she said, beaming. "The one with quintuplets in her family."

I could have died.

"How exciting," Noel's father replied. "It must be hectic, having five little ones in the house."

"But Natalie doesn't mind, do you, dear?" Michelle's mom said. "She's a regular little mother's helper." I don't know where she got her facts. She'd never even been in our house.

After the rest of the introductions we were allowed to go off to the TV room.

"Sorry about all that," Noel murmured.

"It's okay," I said.

But the party had been ruined for me. No one ever said anymore, "Oh Natalie, you're so nice or so bright," or so whatever. All they ever said now was, "Oh Natalie, you're the one with quints in the family!" It wasn't fair. *I was more than just the sister of the quints*. Wasn't I?

Books by Stella Pevsner

AND YOU GIVE ME A PAIN, ELAINE
CUTE IS A FOUR-LETTER WORD
LINDSAY, LINDSAY, FLY AWAY HOME
SISTER OF THE QUINTS

Available from ARCHWAY Paperbacks

ME, MY GOAT, AND MY SISTER'S WEDDING

Available from MINSTREL Books

SISTER OF THE QUINTS

STELLA PEVSNER

AN ARCHWAY PAPERBACK
Published by POCKET BOOKS
New York   London   Toronto   Sydney   Tokyo

An Archway Paperback published by
POCKET BOOKS, a division of Simon & Schuster, Inc.
1230 Avenue of the Americas, New York, N.Y. 10020

Copyright © 1987 by Stella Pevsner
Cover artwork copyright © 1988 Robert Tanenbaum

Published by arrangement with Clarion Books
Library of Congress Catalog Card Number: 86-17565

ISBN: 0-671-65973-1

First Archway Paperback printing May 1988

10 9 8 7 6 5 4 3 2 1

AN ARCHWAY PAPERBACK and colophon are registered trademarks of Simon & Schuster, Inc.

Printed in the U.S.A.

IL 7+

For
Josephine, Florence,
John, Carl, and Donald,
my brothers and sisters
(but not quints)

SISTER OF THE QUINTS

1

———o■o■o———

I don't know how Claudia does it. From the way she was chugging around the field, you'd swear soccer was the only thing on her little eighth-grade mind. But when she got the ball up close enough to pass to me, she yelled, "Who's the guy?"

After I'd slammed the ball across to Jiggs I yelled back, "What guy?"

"Up there with Michelle. Do we know him?" As I stood there straining to see the distance through my new soft lenses, Claudia shouted, "Get it, Natalie!" And because I didn't, the coach yelled, "Wake up, Wentworth!"

After that, I paid such total attention I forgot about the guy up in the stands with Michelle until we broke after the third quarter.

"Wow, just look at him!" Claudia said as we jogged back toward the bench. "I've got to get a close-up. Hey, Michelle!" She waved. Michelle waved back and started toward us. The guy came along with her.

1

"How do I look? Grungy and sweaty?" Claudia took a quick sniff in the direction of her underarms.

"You look and smell like any other player at this stage of the game," Jiggs commented.

"I do not. I'm revolting in my own special way."

We laughed, but I knew very well that Claudia wasn't exactly kidding. She has this conviction that the world has never experienced anyone remotely like her. Maybe it hasn't. Anyway, I'm pretty sure there's no one in our galaxy who goes by her nickname . . . willingly. Claudia, whose last name is Traine, adores being called Choo Choo.

"Oh, just look at him," Choo Choo was all but moaning now, as we neared the bench. "Tall, dark, and break-your-heart gorgeous."

"He looks undernourished to me," Jiggs commented. Jiggs is on the sturdy side and leans toward beefy guys, guys who can provide a challenge in Indian wrestling.

"Not undernourished," Claudia said under her breath. "More like lean and mysterious. Hi, Michelle!"

"Hi, *jocks,*" Michelle said. The word sounded a little off, coming from someone so picture-pretty. Michelle is, in fact, a model, whose picture appears fairly often in sales catalogs. "You're lookin' good out there." It came out a bit wistful. Michelle's mother has put the lid on extracurricular sports ever since last year when Michelle got clobbered on the chin with a hockey stick. You can hardly see the scar, though.

"Who's your friend?" Choo Choo asked right out.

"Oh . . ." Michelle gave him a fast look. "This is

2

Noel. And this is Jiggs . . . I mean Jennifer, and Natalie and Claudia."

"Everyone calls me Choo Choo," Claudia said, smiling.

"*Ah choo,* did you say?" the guy asked. "As in sneeze?"

"No, *Choo Choo.* As in Traine. My last name."

"Ah. Choo Choo Traine." He seemed to be enjoying this. "And Jennifer . . . Jiggs." He looked at me. "And you, Natalie, what are you called?"

"Just Natalie."

"Natalie." The way he said it, I felt a little flickering flame. In just a moment Choo Choo had blown it out.

"Natalie has quints," is what she said. I wanted to kick her.

"Quints?" Noel looked puzzled. "What are quints?"

"You know, babies. Five of them."

"But . . . babies?"

Choo Choo's laugh rang out. "Not Natalie. Her mother. Her *mother* has five babies."

Despite my embarrassment, I managed to mutter, "*Step*mother."

"Oh. Like our Dionnes," Noel said.

"Our what?" Jiggs asked, scowling a little.

"The five babies born in Canada, a long time ago," he said. "Haven't you ever heard of the Dionnes?"

The conversation had drifted too far from Choo Choo's control so she hauled it closer with, "And what brings you to our humble little soccer game?"

"I wanted to look at the fields," Noel said. "I may try out. If it's not too late."

"It's never too late for an ace player," Choo Choo said. "Are you an ace?"

Noel laughed. The thing I noticed about him right away was his easiness. He didn't get all red-faced the way some of the guys do around girls. "I know the game," he said. "We play a lot in Canada."

I was dying to know who he really was and why he was here, and for how long, but I wasn't about to act all that interested. In a few minutes we had to go out for the last quarter. As we trotted off I glanced back and saw him leaving with Michelle.

"What a hunk!" Claudia exclaimed. "And from Canada, too! Trust Michelle to snap him right up."

"I still think he looks on the puny side," Jiggs said. "But he may be fast on the field."

"What did you think of him, Nat?" Choo Choo asked, giving me a sidelong look.

"Please, for the hundred umpteenth time, don't call me Nat."

"Okay. So what did you think of him, Na-ta-lie?"

"Nothing."

"Oh come on, what's the matter? Did I say or do something?"

"I just want to finish the game and get it over with." Of course she'd said something. Choo Choo never misses a chance to drag the quints into a conversation, if the focus happens to be shifting away from her. You'd think they were some kind of product and she was their sponsor.

As the game continued, my concentration just wasn't there. After a couple of fumbles, I got replaced. Coach Collins didn't actually say anything, but I wondered, as I went over to the bench, if this would work against me during the upcoming basketball tryouts.

Collins is a tall, stocky guy with blond hair and a mustache. He likes to kid around if things are going okay, but he can be tough, too. He never misses a move. For example, he'll make little digs if the boyfriends of the players hang around. I noticed it was okay, though, when his own girlfriend came out and watched. She was there now, Ms. Bredlow, the school psychologist. Most of us thought she was too classy for Collins, but there's probably a man shortage here in the suburbs, or else there's a side to the coach that we don't know about.

In my irritable frame of mind, I was hoping Ms. Bredlow wouldn't notice me or come over to talk, but she did.

"Well, Natalie," she said, settling on the bench beside me, "it's nice to see you again. Of course, I've seen you, but not to talk to. How are things going in your life?"

"Oh, just fine." I gave her a quick smile. She was smiling, too. She's quite pretty, with huge brown eyes that light up when she's happy or become like a sorrowful doe's when she's concerned about something. Her hair is brown and full and she's got a neat figure. As I said, she looks too good for Coach Collins.

"How's your mother, Natalie?"

I hesitated. Did she mean my real mother or Jean? I hated it when people referred to Jean as my mother.

She cleared it up by adding, "Did you get out to Colorado Springs to see her this last summer?"

"Yes. I went out in August. I was supposed to go out in July but . . ." I hesitated. "I couldn't."

5

"Oh. Tell me, is she still happy about living out there?"

"She says she is."

"But misses you, I'm sure."

"Well, she's getting used to it. She's been away for more than a year now.

"That long?" Ms. Bredlow put a hand on my wrist. "And are *you* used to it, Natalie? Having your mother so far away?"

I wished she'd stop the questions. I slipped my hand from her touch by leaning down and pulling at my sock. "She's not so far away if you think of it as three hours by plane, rather than the number of miles."

"What a good idea. And it's lucky your father's a pilot. You can probably fly to Colorado whenever you choose."

"Right." I didn't bother to mention that my father had quit being a pilot and was working in the airline office now. Actually, it didn't make that much difference. I could still fly almost for free.

"Still, visiting your mother can't be the same as living with her."

Why was Ms. Bredlow doing this to me? Was she so concerned or just curious? "I don't know anyone out there," I said. "Except for my mother, of course, and a couple of her friends."

"No kids your own age to run around with?" And then, teasing, "Not any cute guys?"

I laughed. "No. I was supposed to meet two girls in July, but when I didn't get there until August, they were away, camping." Shifting on the bench, I went on, "Anyway, I've got good friends here. I'd miss Choo Choo and Jiggs if I left. Michelle, too."

6

The image of Noel flickered in my mind. Maybe he could be another reason to stay. But that was crazy. He'd already latched on to Michelle. Then I realized Ms. Bredlow had said something. "Sorry. What did you say?"

"I asked if you'd miss the quints. You would, wouldn't you?"

"Sure. Like I'd miss the measles."

The counselor gave her pleasant, tinkly laugh. "Oh, now, Natalie, they're adorable and you know it."

"I know they're becoming pests. They're crawling around like crazy and two have started to walk. We had to put gates at the stairway and even across the doorway to their room."

"They must keep your . . . their mother . . . hopping."

"Yeh. All of us." I strained forward to watch the action at the other end of the field. Choo Choo had the ball and a clear shot at the goal and then—and then that Trish Mandrake had to barge in and take over, and louse it all up. "What a jerk!" I muttered. "Whose side is she on, anyway?"

Ms. Bredlow seemed confused. "What happened?"

"Oh, just Miss Know-It-All. . . . nothing."

Coach Collins blew his whistle, yelled something I couldn't hear, and then Trish came toward the bench, scowling. When she got close enough, she yelled to me, "He wants you in." And then she had to add, "We're losing anyway."

What a sleaze! As though she'd had nothing to do with messing up that shot. I got up, and said, "See you later, Ms. Bredlow."

"Sure. And Natalie . . ."

I turned. "Yes?"

"I'm glad things are working out for you."

"Thanks." I was glad to be getting away from her. If we'd gone on talking, I might have broken down and told her things actually weren't working out. Since I'd gotten back from Mother's, life at home had become one big series of problems . . . for me, for Jean, and for Dad.

Jogging out to the field, I tried to put all that out of my mind. Right now, I was going to concentrate on reversing the score. After that, I could go back to brooding about things at home.

"Yay, Natalie. Come on, let's clobber them!" Jiggs yelled as I took up position.

"Yeh, let's do it!" I yelled back.

At least in soccer you knew the moves and knew the score. It was a lot easier than everyday life. Easier to deal with and a whole lot easier to understand. And when the game was over, you could put it out of your mind. Not like the situation at home. It just went on and on, getting a little bit worse each day.

2

○■○■○

After the game I was in the locker room, bending over and trying to tie a knot in a broken shoelace. A pair of legs appeared in front of me, and on those legs were panty hose in the vilest shade of pink I've ever seen. It could only be Trish.

"Move out of my light, will you?" I muttered, not even looking up.

She moved about a quarter of an inch. "So who was the guy with Miss Montgomery Ward Model?"

I straightened up. "If you mean Michelle, why don't you ask her?"

"Because I'm asking *you*."

What a clever comeback. "Well, go ask her anyway. Move, will you, Trish? You're not exactly a window."

"Though you are a bit of a pane," Choo Choo said, strolling up. "Thanks a lot, Trish, for lousing up what could have been an easy score out there."

"Oh, sure, blame me." Trish stalked away.

Choo Choo made a growling sound, and then asked me what Trish had wanted.

9

I got up and stowed my stuff in the locker. "She wanted to know about the guy with Michelle."

"What did you tell her?"

"Nothing." I slammed the locker door and twisted the combination. "Let's get out of here. This place seems to smell worse every day. All the stale sweat and stuff."

Jiggs had already taken off. Choo Choo and I went outside and walked together for a bit. It was still early October but the weather was getting brisk. Before we quite reached the corner where our paths separate, Choo Choo stopped.

"What is it?" I asked, stopping too.

"Did Trish say anything about . . ." And then Choo Choo put her hand over her mouth. "Oh, I guess I shouldn't mention it."

"What? Mention what?" I could see she was dying to tell me.

Although there was no one near, Choo Choo lowered her voice. "You've a right to know. There's a rumor going around that Trish and Troy are like that." To demonstrate, she held up her hand with two fingers pressed together.

"So?"

"So I thought you might want to do something about it."

I gave Choo Choo a steady look. "Why should I want to do something about it? I don't like Troy anymore. You know that."

"Yes, but do you want Trish to have him? And spoil all your marvelous romantic memories?"

"Claudia, come on. I wish you wouldn't make it sound as though the earth moved or something. Troy

10

and I just hung out together at school last year. That's all there was to it."

Claudia, lifting her chin, looked off into the distance. "Very well, if you intend to be noble and high-minded about it."

If it had been anyone else, I'd have been annoyed, but I knew how Choo Choo loved being dramatic.

"Thanks for telling me, anyway," I said. "Now if anyone mentions it I'll just look bored and say, 'So what else is new?' "

"Good." Placated, Choo Choo asked if I wanted to come over to her house for a while.

I shifted the books in my arms. "I wish I could, but I've got to get home. You know, this is the toughest time of day for the sitter. When the quints get up from their naps they're full of energy. We've got a new woman now . . . our fifth one since Jean went back to work. If this sitter leaves, I don't know who we'll get next."

"Natalie, you say 'we' as if it's your problem. It isn't, though. Just because Jean and your dad had that litter, it doesn't mean you have to give up your life to help baby-sit."

The fact that Choo Choo was right didn't make me feel any better. "They don't expect anything from me," I alibied, "but I feel I should at least pitch in."

"Oh, all right." Choo Choo's mood shifted. "Aren't you dying to find out more about that guy . . . Noel? I think I'll give Michelle a call."

"Good idea. Let me know what you find out."

"For sure. Ta!" Choo Choo said, with a wave of her fingers, the way some English guy did in a movie we saw. "I'll call you tonight."

11

While walking the four blocks home, I found myself thinking of Noel, and replaying the meeting in my mind. I could still see his smile when he asked Choo Choo about her name. And I could hear his voice saying my own. Nat-a-lie. No, more like Not-ah-lee. He made it sound so special, like a word in a poem. Not-ah-lee and Noel. They went so well together. And then I realized what I was doing . . . fantasizing about a guy I'd barely met. *Wimp,* I told myself, *he's a friend of Michelle's. And Michelle's a friend, too. So stop this right now!*

I made myself think of my math assignment. My mind didn't want to dwell on that subject. It never did. So I thought about English lit, but I'd have to look up my notes to see what it was that I was supposed to be reading.

By the time I reached my front door, my mind had revolved to what it wanted to think about. Noel. It didn't stay there for long, though. In less than a minute I was in the house and in the direct path of the toddler tornado.

"Lee, Lee!" one of the babies screeched. He headed for me on all fours, his little diapered bottom waggling back and forth from the action. And then the others came at me like those crazy cars that go every which way at a carnival.

"Now, children, settle down!" The sitter, Mrs. Hinley, clucked like a hen but the chicks ignored her.

"Cool it, you guys," I shouted over the screeches. "Give me a break!"

Now they were hanging on me from all sides. I was afraid of falling over, so I dropped my books, purse, everything, and started detaching little quint hands.

12

" 'Sey," one of them yelled, and the others chimed in, " 'Sey, 'sey!" What a racket.

"I'll give you horsey-back rides later," I said, pulling away again. "Natalie has to go upstairs now." I scrabbled for my stuff, bolted to the stairs, tossed my things over the extension gate, opened it, closed it behind me and started up the stairs. The quints, hot on my trail, started shaking the gate almost off its hinges, howling all the while like coyotes. Well, too bad.

As I reached the top of the stairs, the howling suddenly stopped. Looking down, I saw Mrs. Hinley reaching into her pocket and fishing out cookies. Wow. Did she pass them around all day? Jean would have a fit if she knew. I'd never tell, though. Anything to keep the peace.

I was tempted, after I'd changed clothes, to put on my headphones and just stay upstairs until Jean or Dad got home. I couldn't, though. Even though the quints were a pack of trouble, I had to feel sorry for them, cooped in all day with a woman who kept saying, "Now, children! . . ."

When I ambled downstairs, Mrs. Hinley was in the nursery with the babies. This used to be our living room before quint time, known as the B.Q. period. She was playing peek-a-boo with one of the kids. Another looked on. One crawled around and around the easy chair and another hit him each time he circled.

I ran over the names of the four present—Alice, Emma, Beth, Craig. "Where's Drew?" I asked Mrs. Hinley.

"Drew, did you say?"

"Yes, Drew. One of the babies." Really!

13

"Oh! Well . . ." She looked around. "He must surely be here someplace. My goodness. I don't see him."

I wondered if Jean had checked this woman's credentials.

"Never mind, I'll find him," I said.

I checked the stairs gate. It was fastened, and I didn't think Drew could climb over it. I looked in the parents' bedroom (which used to be the TV room in the B.Q. period). The closet door was closed. Under the bed? Yes. There he was, under the bed.

"Drew . . . come on Drew." I took hold of one of his chubby arms, but I couldn't slide him toward me because of the shag carpet.

"Hey, Drewsie . . . come on, baby."

It was dim under there, but I could still see his little lips pucker and the tears start. "Ma . . . ma," he whimpered.

"Mama will be home soon. Come with Natalie." I gave a tiny tug but he pulled his hand away. Now he began to wail, "Ma . . . ma!"

"Shhh. It's all right." I wondered if they cried for Jean a lot.

Suddenly I felt a hand on my ankle, which was sticking out from under the bed. "Natalie? What in heaven's name is going on?"

Dad. Good. I wriggled out backward and explained, "Drew's under there, but he just wants his mama."

"I'll try." Dad took my place and shimmied under the bed. In half a second he was wriggling back out, and Drew was coming out with him. Once clear of the bed, Drew wrapped his arms around Dad's neck and quietly sobbed.

14

"Poor little fellow," Dad soothed. "It's all right now. Daddy's here. Daddy knows what to do."

"I'm so glad Daddy knows," I told him. "No one else does."

"All it takes is a little patience, and kindness," Dad said.

"Wonderful." I gave him a look and left. I really wanted to point out that it's easy enough to be patient and kind for an hour or so a day, but just try doing it for an eight-hour stretch, the way I had done part of the time last summer. I didn't say it though, because Dad and I weren't getting along all that well and I didn't want to start anything.

3

○■○■○

When I reached my room I flopped across the bed. I could hear various sounds downstairs, then a car, and then Jean's voice and then another car—Mrs. Hinley leaving.

I knew I should go downstairs to help but I thought, *Oh let them deal with it. Daddy's here. Daddy knows what to do.*

I reached over and put a Madonna tape into the player.

Compared with being around the quints, anything from Madonna to heavy metal rock was soothing. It used to be different. When I lived with Mom right after the divorce, I used to play tapes partly to fill the silence.

My mother was gone a lot of the time, to teachers' meetings or to various adult classes. She was high on self-improvement and keeping up on things. She even took a computer literacy course, not because she was all that crazy about electronics, but because she didn't want her high school students to know something she didn't. That computer course wasn't easy for her, but she wouldn't give up. That's the way my mother is about learning. It used to drive her up the wall when I'd say, "I can't" or "It's too much work." Once she slipped and said I sounded just like my father.

That wasn't fair, and I told her so, pointing out that Dad had gone through pilots' training and made a success of it. I suppose Mom could have come back with, "And what has he done since then?" but she didn't. I have to say that Mother is basically a very fair and decent person, though firm in her ways. She would never try to turn me against my own father. Whatever she felt about the divorce and his really quick marriage to Jean, she never said anything about it, at least not to me.

If Dad had married just anyone, I'd probably have felt bitter, but Jean was something else. She really liked me, I could tell. She talked to me like a good friend, not as a stepmother. And on weekends, when I usually went over to their house (the same one where Mom and Dad and I used to live), she always had plans that included me.

Where Mom tends to move about quietly and do things without any fuss, Jean is all energy. I never knew what to expect on Saturdays when I went over. One week Jean might be painting a room or helping Dad build shelves. The next week it might be racquetball down at the courts or camping out. We all registered for scuba diving lessons so we could go to Jamaica or maybe Cancun, where they say the undersea sights are fantastic. No matter what we did, Jean always made it seem like an adventure.

Naturally, I didn't mention any of this to Mother. I

guess she could tell, though, that I really enjoyed hanging around Dad and his new wife.

I didn't even mind when Jean told me, sometime in February of last year, that she was pregnant. I just imagined myself as the big sister of a sweet little angel girl who would grow up to love and admire me as I loved and admired Jean. I didn't go beyond the dream image, to think of the baby as a *person*.

A couple of months later, when we heard it wasn't to be a baby, but two, or even more, I was as excited as Jean and Dad. *What a lark,* I thought. *The three of us with a bundle of babies!*

Mom's reaction, when I told her, was quite different. At first she looked shocked, and then somewhat aghast. "Good lord," she finally said, "how will your father be able to cope with all that?"

I felt a bit let down. "Aren't you excited?" I said, without thinking.

She just looked at me. "Should I be?"

Then I realized, of course, that it wasn't the greatest thing in the world for her. In fact, it could even be a bit embarrassing when it became known that her former husband and his wife were expecting triplets.

It was around May, I think, when we found out that the babies were going to be quintuplets. Jean and Dad seemed awed and a little scared at this development. I didn't know what to think. As for Mother, she made plans.

Not long after Dad told her about the newest count of babies, my mom announced that she was going to move. Dumb me. I thought she meant to another house. I found out she meant to move to another state.

Colorado, to be exact. She'd gotten a new teaching job there.

When she broke the news to me, I burst into tears.

"Darling, what's the matter?" she asked. "I thought you'd be happy and excited."

"But I'll miss you," I said, still crying.

She looked baffled. "Miss me? But you'll be going along, of course."

I stared at her, shocked. My tears gave way to indignation. "To Colorado? You must be crazy!" (I shouldn't have said that, of course. It made things worse.) "I'm staying here, no matter what *you* do."

"Young lady," Mother said, "you'll do as you're told. You're still not grown-up, no matter what impression you may have gotten from *them*."

That did it. "If you mean Jean and Dad, they treat me like a human being, not a little kid. You're just jealous because they're happy and they make me happy, too."

For a moment, I thought Mom was going to slap me for the very first time. She didn't, though. Much later on, I wished she had. Then maybe I wouldn't have felt so rotten when I remembered the scene.

All she did was give me a look I'll never forget, and then she went off to her room. An hour or so passed and she still hadn't come out. Finally, I knocked on the door and asked her about dinner. She said I could have whatever I wanted, she wasn't hungry. I cased the refrigerator and freezer, but nothing appealed to me, not even the Häagen-Dazs ice cream I normally love. I ended up munching this and that and then going off to my own room.

When I told Jean and Dad that Mother was going to

move, Jean assumed that I'd have to go with her. "Oh, babe," she cried out, "not all the way to Colorado! That's miles from here."

"Natalie's not going," Dad said. Just like that.

"I'm not?" I was overjoyed. "You've talked to Mom?"

"Not yet," Dad said, "but I will." Even though he was angry, when Dad set his lips like that the dimples showed. With his curly brown hair (that was going a bit gray) and his "wicked brown eyes," as Jean called them, he was a handsome guy. He looked good even now, angry as he was.

"What'll you do, Dad?" I asked.

"Never mind." And then he said, "I'm going to have a talk with Isobel, that's what I'm going to do."

"Jack, now, be nice," Jean urged. I think Jean was just a little in awe of my mother. "This can't be easy for her."

"Easy for her? What about the rest of us?" When Dad's temper started rising I always got uneasy. To try to calm him down, I said, "Maybe Mom will change her mind."

Dad looked at me. "Have you ever known your mother to do that?"

"Well . . . no.'

"We have joint custody, as you know," Dad said to Jean. "That doesn't give Isobel the right to drag Natalie out of state. She's not going to, either."

I never was told what went on between Mom and Dad, but I guess they talked to a lawyer. The upshot of it all was that I didn't have to go to Colorado unless I chose to do so.

I chose to stay. I don't even want to think about

what that did to Mom. She didn't get angry or yell or anything. She just looked terribly sad. It seemed to me that the bright blue of her eyes faded a little, and even the gentle blond of her hair, that I'd always regretted not inheriting, seemed to wash out, too. But it was mostly her expression that seemed to change. Suddenly the firm look wasn't there at all. I wanted to put my arms around her and tell her I loved her and would go with her, but I didn't. I just didn't. I guess the reaction I knew my dad would have if I told him kept me from changing my mind.

Mom left in July. I moved back to my old house, to my old room that I'd been using only on weekends this past year. After a while it seemed perfectly natural to be the daughter of the house where I'd lived before, only this time without the old tension.

Jean kept getting bigger and bigger. Finally, to keep from having the babies before they were ready, she had to stay in bed. If she felt bad at times, she didn't let on. We spent a lot of time—Dad and I—in the room with her, watching movies on the VCR Dad had bought, or sometimes looking at travel folders, planning trips. Only now it was for "some day" way in the future.

My phone rang, bringing me back to the present. I grabbed it, wondering if Choo Choo had had time to grill Michelle about that Noel. It was only Dad on the other line, announcing that dinner was ready and they'd be honored if I'd join them. He was kidding, but at the same time I knew he wanted me downstairs. Now.

When I got to the bottom of the stairs and was refastening the gate behind me, Jean came out of their

21

room. She'd already changed to jeans and a floppy shirt, her standard gear around the house.

She gave me a quick hug and asked, "How did practice go today, sweetie?"

"Fair." It was funny. Jean always asked about sports and seldom schoolwork. Mother had considered sports as merely a breather between sessions of study.

"The soccer season's almost over," I said, "so tryouts for basketball will be . . ." I stopped talking because Jean wasn't beside me. I turned and saw her scooping up Beth, no, Alice, and with a quick motion pulling something out of her mouth.

"You little stinker," Jean said, "where did you get that penny?" She flipped it into a vase, and with Alice on her hip continued with me to the kitchen.

"Oh, here you are," Dad said to Jean. "And you found Alice. I was about to go look for her."

Jean crammed the protesting baby into her high chair. "Sit, Fido!" she said. Alice scooted as far down as she could, and then pumped her legs up and down and started squealing. Jean hoisted her back in place.

"Here." Dad gave the baby a cracker. Alice whacked it on the rim of the feeder and then, seeing the bits, stopped squealing. She turned her attention to the job of smashing the bits with the palm of her hand until they were ground into crumbs. The other quints looked on with great interest. Dad began going "Boom, boom, boom!" each time Alice's fist came down.

In the meantime, Jean dished up the quints' food on five little plastic plates with blue elephants bopping around the rims.

22

"You'd better cool the 'boom-boom' business now," she said to Dad, "or this stuff will start flying all over the kitchen."

Dinner tonight was going to be what I called a Thomas Paine Special, because he once wrote, "These are the times that try men's souls." Eating with the quints was trying in several ways. You tried not to notice the mess they made. You tried not to be in their line of fire. You tried not to barf. I would recommend a steady routine of eating with the quints to anyone who wants to lose weight in a hurry.

Fortunately, we didn't always eat together. On the days that Dad came home early, he'd put together something we could just heat up after the quints had been fed, bathed, and bottled for the night. Dad's hours at the airline office are somewhat irregular, but not nearly as bad as when he was a pilot. Back then, he'd sometimes have to fly at night and sleep during the day. Changing to an office job meant a cut in salary, though, and it meant that Jean had to go back to work, too. They both worked for the same airline, but in different buildings.

Since this was one of Dad's longer workdays, we all ate together, more or less, with such sparkling dinner conversation as, "Watch out, he's dumping it on the floor!" "Oh, Alice, not in your hair!" "No, Bethie, eat your own food . . . now sit up!"

At first, I used to try to remove myself mentally from the table, as I sometimes do during health lectures at school. But you had to be more or less alert here to keep from getting food-bombed.

"Anything new at work?" Dad asked Jean. "Stop . . . no! Drew!"

23

"Remember Sylvia, the stew who sometimes worked your Dallas flights?"

"Yeh I think so, the one with red hair and a terminal case of cuteness?"

"That's the one. Well, she's—No, Alice, no patty-cake! Here, eat this—she's getting married again. Third time, but who's counting?"

"Did she meet this one in Dallas, too?"

"I guess."

I tuned out. I hated this kind of gossip about people I didn't even know. They never used to yak about stuff like this around me, but now they had so little time together that they caught up on shop talk whenever they could.

Jean finally realized how bored I was. "So, Natalie, how did the game go today?"

"Okay. Pretty soon now we're going to have basketball tryouts."

"Great," Jean said. "I'll bet you make the team."

"I'm not so sure. There's lots of competition."

"Maybe it would be better if you cut down on sports for a while," Dad said.

"Why would I do that?"

"Well . . . to . . . to give yourself time for other things."

Like what, I wanted to say. *Like hurrying home to baby-sit?*

I might have actually said it, but just then Alice, like a pitcher at the mound, aimed a fastball of mashed potatoes at Dad. He ducked, and the stuff splattered all over the back of his chair.

"Yay, Alice, good going," I said. "Right over the batter's box."

Reaching to the sink for a clean-up sponge, Dad said, "Very funny, Natalie. Keep egging them on. That'll be a real help."

I was only kidding, but wasn't that just like Dad? To get annoyed at me, but not at his little darlings?

More and more I was realizing that, to my father, I wasn't so much a daughter as free household help. *Get home early. Cut down on sports*. Those were the things he was saying more and more often.

I didn't have to take that. I didn't have to turn over my life to this houseful of babies. I could pack up any time I pleased and go to Mother's. If things kept on this way, I was going to do it, too. Then, suddenly, Dad would realize how unfair he'd been to his eldest, hardworking and uncomplaining daughter. But it would be too late. I'd be gone. Forever.

4

———○■○■○———

I was back in my room, reading my lit assignment, when the phone rang.

"It's me," Choo Choo said.

"It's *I*, ignoramus," I said.

"Do you want to instruct me in grammar or do you want the scoop of the century?"

"I'll take the scoop. Vanilla."

"Dahling, you're so witty. Well!" Choo Choo lapsed into her normal voice. "I called Michelle about Noel and if I may say so, handled it very well."

"You may say so. Who is he and why is he here?"

"His family is a friend of Michelle's family from way back when someone, I forget just who, lived in Canada."

"Why are they moving here?"

"Oh, who cares why. Get this—Noel lives just down the street from you!"

"All *right!*"

"Oh, but don't get your hopes up," Choo Choo said. "He's definitely Michelle's."

26

"She told you that?" It didn't sound like Michelle.

"No, pea brain. It's just so obvious. If you were a guy, wouldn't you flip over a looker like Michelle?"

I almost pointed out that the guys at school didn't, but I knew why. They were a little in awe of her. And she was too shy to make any kind of approach herself. With Noel, though, none of that would matter since they had a built-in family friendship.

"Dear Noel's a whiz at sports, I understand," Choo Choo went on. "He's sure to make the team. His father was some kind of champion in the Olympics in his day."

"Have you changed your mind about trying out for basketball?" I said, switching the subject. "I wish you would. Jiggs is."

"Oh, please, Jiggs is the natural athletic type. I am not." Choo Choo sighed. "I realize more and more each day that my métier is possibly the theater."

"In other words, you don't think you'd make the team anyway." I'm about the only person who can talk to Claudia that way and live to tell about it.

She laughed. "No, I probably wouldn't make the team. But only because I'm not dedicated. Do you think you'll make it?"

"I'd guess I have a fifty-fifty chance."

"Oh, come on. Collins likes you. He always has. You're his little golden girl."

"Not anymore. I've goofed up a lot lately." I didn't want to go on about it to Choo Choo, but I was thinking it wasn't only the coach I had to consider, but also Dad. The way things were now, he was either going to keep me from taking part, or he'd let me and

27

then make me feel guilty every time I came home late
from practice.

I found out that Noel not only lived near me, but
also had his locker just about ten away from mine. I
saw him there the next day after the last class, when
the hall was otherwise empty.

My heart gave a flip as he noticed me, smiled and
walked over. "Hi, Natalie." (It came out *Not-ah-lee*
again.)

"Hi." I couldn't say his name. I was afraid I'd give
away the fact that I'd said it aloud to myself several
times. "How do you like the school here so far?" Not
brilliant, but I had to say something.

"The school?" He smiled and shrugged. "Like any
other."

"Yeh. Uh. Well, how do you like the subjects so
far?" I am generally known as a girl with a quick
comeback, but now my brain was practically para-
lyzed.

"The subjects?" His smile was wide now, showing
teeth that had probably never been trapped in metal.
"I'll describe them in detail as we walk home together."

"Oh." So we were walking together. "Okay."

Fortunately, considering my comatose state, Noel
did most of the talking, and that was mostly about
sports. He didn't so much as mention the quints. Had
he forgotten, or did he consider babies a boring subject? All too soon, we were in front of my house, and
with a cheerful, "So long," he continued on his way.
He didn't even glance back as I stood rooted to the

28

spot. So okay, I was nothing more than a neighbor. I could live with that. For the time being.

I was glad he hadn't hung around, though, once I got to the house. As I opened the door I heard a huge *bump* and *thump* and then a deafening howl.

"For Pete's sake, Natalie, can't you be careful?" Dad yelled, coming over to pick up the screaming Craig.

"How was I supposed to know he was standing there?"

"You do know they live here and are running around." Dad kissed the baby's head and tried to shush him.

"How come you're home? Where's Mrs. Hinley?"

"Her husband injured his back and she had to go to the medical center. Just what we need."

"Isn't she coming back?"

"How should I know?" Dad set Craig down. "I had to rush home right in the middle of a big job. Now I'll have to go back for a couple of hours. I was waiting for you." From his tone, you'd think I'd deliberately taken my time.

"Couldn't Jean get away?"

"She was in a meeting." Dad reached for his jacket. "She may be in line for a promotion. Let's hope so." He put on the leather jacket from his pilot days and started out. "Oh. Try to stay off the phone until Jean gets home, will you? You can't take your eyes off the quints for a second."

"Don't worry. And I'll keep them away from the door." I wanted to add, *as you should have done,* but didn't.

He left.

Looking around, I could see that Dad had been no better at keeping order in the room than Mrs. Hinley. Clothes baskets were upturned and toys were scattered all over. At the moment, Drew, the swiftest of the quints, was trying to climb the shelves of the built-in bookcase. Before long they'd all be swinging like Tarzan from the very top.

You'd never know, by looking at the babies now, that they'd been skinny, delicate little things at birth. Jiggs had summed up their looks pretty well. "If they were fish, you'd have to throw them back, they're so undersized," she said.

I began picking up clothes, folding them, and putting them back onto what had once been our bookshelves. I wondered if Jean would have taken those fertility pills if she'd guessed she'd have so many babies. Her first marriage was—and these were her words, not mine—*a disaster*. "I'm just thankful there were no children involved," she'd said. But if her marriage to Dad was the next thing to perfect, why did she have to mess it up by having children? In my opinion, they were the disaster this time.

Next, I started throwing toys back into the baskets, but it was a lost cause. The quints reached down and tossed them out again. I turned at the sounds of a struggle behind me.

"Drew!" I snapped, "Leave that teddy bear alone! It's Emma's!" I tried to pull him away, but he set up a howl. I picked up Emma instead, and when she squirmed around to try to get the teddy, I took an identical one off the shelf for her. She flung it away.

I found it hard to believe that I'd once thought these little pests were adorable. But they were tiny then,

30

and stayed where you put them. I can even remember wishing the volunteer help would leave so I could hold one of the babies and give it a bottle. What a fool I'd been then. And what a bigger fool to choose to stay here, when I could have gone to a life of freedom and fun at Mother's!

A tiny scream punctured my thoughts. It was two of the girls this time.

"Alice, stop that!" I shouted, unclenching her fingers from Beth's hair. I guess I yelled too loud, because Alice began to cry, Beth added her voice, and the rest joined in the chorus.

How long had I been back from Mother's? I was there in August, so it was only about six weeks. It seemed like a century. "Mother," I murmured now, "why didn't you just insist that I stay this time? What kind of mother are you, anyway, to listen to a demented daughter?"

Mother had asked me to stay, but for the second time, I'd chosen to live with Dad.

The visit with Mom hadn't been too great, anyway. It got off to a bad start when I couldn't go in July, as originally planned.

Two things had happened at home. Jean had come down with a virus that just wouldn't go away, and then the littlest quint, Emma, had become quite ill. At first the doctor thought Jean had something really serious. It wasn't, but then Emma, too, got sick for a long time . . . and she would have nothing to do with the sitter. If she couldn't have her mother, she wanted me, and only me. I knew it was important for me to be there, even if it meant changing my plans with Mother.

Mother hadn't felt that way.

31

When Dad was about to call her he told me to get on the extension phone and "back him up." He must have guessed Mother wouldn't take the postponement too well. She didn't. In fact, she was furious.

"You're asking me to change all my plans out here, Jack, to accommodate you and your family?"

"Look, Isobel, whatever your plans are, they can surely be altered. We're in a bind, here. We need Natalie's help."

"I don't consider my daughter hired help, and you'd better not, either."

Hired? I thought. *Since when do I get paid?*

"What are those plans of yours, anyway, that are suddenly so important?" Dad asked Mom. "Has the governor invited you to his ski lodge or what?"

"I don't know the governor and we don't ski out here in summer," Mom snapped back. (Actually, she never skied at any time.) "A friend and her two daughters have invited Natalie and me to spend some time at a dude ranch. The girls could go riding, and there'd be other activities I know Natalie would love. It's not fair to deprive her of all that."

"Can't you do it later?"

"No. There's just this particular time available. I'll have to cancel out if there's to be a delay."

A pause followed. Then Dad said, "Natalie's on the other phone. Natalie, what do you think about all this?"

He really put me on the spot. It wasn't fair. No matter what I said, I'd seem to be siding in with one of them.

When I hesitated, Mother said, "Natalie?"

I didn't want to upset her. But Dad had a point.

They needed me. And if I did go as arranged, I wouldn't really have a good time, wondering how they were getting along at home.

"Mother," I said, "it really sounds good, the dude ranch and all. But maybe we could do it next summer instead? I guess I should wait and come out next month. It'll be nice, just being with you."

I could almost see her face tighten. All she said, though, was, "All right, Natalie. I'll see you next month then."

The quints jolted me back to the present. They were crawling around, butting into each other like a herd of wild goats. It was a real relief to hear Jean's car outside. Rescue at last!

I opened the gate to the room and the babies tore out and swarmed all over Jean as she came inside. "Help! Help!" she cried. "The Munsters are taking over the universe! How you doin', Natalie?" One by one, she picked up the kids, gave them hugs and kisses and then swung them back to the floor. "I left the meeting as soon as I could. Natalie, I really appreciate your taking over."

"That's all right." Jean was always grateful. At least *she* never took me for granted. "Is it okay if I go upstairs now?" I asked. "I'm loaded with homework."

"Oh, babe, you don't need to ask! For heaven's sake . . . you do more than you should, as it is."

"I don't mind." I detached a quint from my right leg and made my getaway.

Up in my room, I changed into red and blue sweats and got out my science book. I wished I'd brought

33

along an apple or something, but I didn't want to descend into that crawling mass of kids again.

As I sat at my desk and opened the book, my thoughts drifted back to the walk home with Noel. Carefully I went over everything he'd said and I'd said. There was nothing at all to give a hint that he was the least bit interested in me as a girl.

Anyway, as Choo Choo had said, he belonged to Michelle. She'd known him first. And she was so great-looking and so sweet any guy would want to be near her. She might not be shy around Noel, if they had known each other a long time.

Michelle herself had moved here only about two years ago, and we'd been friends ever since. Yet sometimes I felt I didn't really know her at all. I'd been over to her house now and then, but she never came here. I couldn't understand why. Every time I'd asked her, she'd made up some excuse. Yet she went to Choo Choo's and Jiggs'. Not often, but some. Could it be that she just didn't like being around babies? Some people felt that way, and I could understand why.

Hungry, hungry, hungry. Maybe a call to Choo Choo would take my mind off my stomach. I got down on the floor, leaned against the bed, and dialed.

"Hi, nit-brain," I said when she answered. "What's goin' on?"

"Nothing really, dahling. What's going on there?"

"Nothing. Guess what. Don't tell anybody, but I walked home with *him*. Noel."

"You did? That's awesome. What did he say?"

"He talked about sports."

34

"Sports? How dull and depressing. What about Michelle? What did he say about her?"

"Not one thing. He didn't even mention her name."

"That's strange, when they're so close." Before I could ask, *How close?* she went on, "It may be that he cherishes her so much he doesn't want to share her with anyone . . . not even in conversation."

"Claudia, come off it. Kids our age aren't all that sentimental."

"Oh no? What about you and Troy?"

"Troy? Can't you get it through your scuzzy brain? Troy and I are history."

"If you say so. I must ring off now. It's chowtime and we're having lasagne."

"Go pig out, then." My stomach rumbled as I hung up. Just what I needed, mention of a great meal like lasagne. We'd probably have some old leftover, like meat loaf.

I remembered the meals we used to have, when there were no quintuplets around to ruin everything. Jean was a great cook, better than Mom ever was, and she liked to try all kinds of ethnic dishes. She'd even try to create a whole atmosphere to go with the food. Like once, she'd strung up Chinese lanterns and had fortune cookies, and even chopsticks, at an Oriental meal. Now we were lucky if we managed to eat a very ordinary meal while it was still hot.

Seriously starving, I went out to the hall and down the stairs very quietly. Could I sneak out to the kitchen, unseen by any quint?

At the foot of the stairs I opened the gate without a sound, went through, and refastened it. Then I heard Jean's voice, softly singing.

35

She and the quints were all sitting on the floor in the quint room, and Jean, with two babes on her lap and her arms around the others, was singing some little song about birdies in their nests.

None of them noticed me as I slithered out to the kitchen. I ate a banana and then bit into a golden delicious apple. The fruit wouldn't spoil my appetite for dinner. There it was, sitting on the counter—the leftover meat loaf.

Another warmed-over meal. That's pretty much the way my whole life seemed these days . . . warmed-over. Nothing new, everything old. Would it ever be fresh and exciting again?

5

○■□■○

Mrs. Hinley (whom I privately called The Cookie Queen) informed Jean one Friday night that she couldn't be there for a while because her son and daughter-in-law were moving to town and she had to help them get settled. Just like that. Two days' notice.

Jean took the news calmly, she was too nice to make a scene, but later she told Dad she was at her wits' end. She didn't know of anyone she could get at this late date.

After Dad went through his usual grumbling routine about the unreliability of people these days, he suddenly snapped his fingers. "How about Toots?"

"Toots?" Jean gave a little click of her tongue. "Oh, Jack, you know how she is."

"Nutty as a fruitcake," Dad commented. "But at least she's family and someone we could count on."

"If she's around," I said. Jean's Aunt Thelma (known as Toots) and her third husband, Horace, owned one of those recreational vehicles called an RV, and they were always on the go. One of their many hobbies was square dancing. Their senior citizens group entered competitions all over the state, and whenever one was going on, Toots and Horace would drive there in the RV and make a mini-vacation of it.

Jean couldn't think of anyone else she could get on such short notice, so she finally called her aunt. Toots said she'd be more than happy to help out.

On Monday, when I got home from practice, I expected to find the house in its usual turmoil. The toys were scattered all over the place as always, but the quints themselves were surprisingly serene.

"What did you do, lace their Jell-O with tranquilizers?" I asked Toots.

"No, kiddo, I just make it a practice to keep one step ahead of the little rascals. The trick is to know what they're going to do before they do it. And then keep them from doing it. Makes sense, doesn't it?"

"Yeh, but what if they all have different ideas and go off in five directions, all at the same time?"

"You don't let them go off in different directions. You keep them in a bunch, like a cowboy herding cattle." Toots scooped up Craig, who had started crawling away, shoved him back with the others, and tossed a few toys into the group to distract them.

Her method worked. For two days. Then the quints began acting worse than ever.

"Girl, I sure am glad to see you," Toots said when I got home on Wednesday. "This bunch wears me out worse than a full night of square dancing."

"You do look beat," I agreed. "The quints'll get to anyone, sooner or later."

Toots hated to admit defeat. "It's not just them," she said. "I've got a tooth that's driving me crazy."

"Shouldn't you see a dentist?"

"Oh, I will, one of these days."

Because Toots was such a good sport who didn't make any demands on me, I tried to get home as soon as possible to help her out.

On Friday, Noel met up with me as I was hurrying up the street. After a bit, he said, "Natalie, you are the fastest-walking girl I've ever known. My mother is always telling me to slow down when I'm with her, and my sister complains, too."

"I didn't know you had a sister," I said. "How old is she?"

"Oh, ancient. She goes to a university in Toronto. So does my older brother." He laughed. "I'm the baby of the family. Don't you pity me?"

"I do not. I'd like to be the youngest in my family. I used to be. The oldest *and* the youngest. Now I'm just another voice in the jungle."

"Cheer up. At least you're your mother's only child. For the time being, anyway."

"What do you mean by that?"

Noel shrugged. "She could get married again, couldn't she?"

What an idea. It had never occurred to me. "She wouldn't! And besides . . ."

He looked down at me as we loped along. "Besides, what?"

"She just wouldn't. And even if she did, she'd never have another child. Why would she?"

"Hey, don't ask me. I don't know your mother." After a pause, he asked, "How long has it been since you've seen her?"

"About six or seven weeks. She calls me every

weekend. And of course, we write all the time.'' That wasn't strictly true. My mother wrote at least once a week. I wrote when I felt like it.

"I really do get lonesome for her," I added, and that was true. I did. "I also miss the peace and quiet I used to have when we lived together. Living with the quints is like . . .''

"Five TVs, tuned to different channels?"

I laughed. "You've got it."

"By the way, do the quints have names, or do they just go by numbers?''

"You're close. They're named for the first five letters of the alphabet."

"How clever. Whose idea was that?"

I cleared my throat in an important-sounding way. "Ta dum!"

He shot me a look. "Yours? I'm impressed. But what exactly are their names?''

"Alice, Beth, Craig, Drew and Emma. Short and sweet, with no two sounding alike. And nothing to make into nicknames. I hate nicknames.''

"How come?"

"I don't know. Maybe because I hate to be called Nat. It makes me think of a bug . . . a gnat.''

"How about Honey? Or Sugar?" He gave a short laugh. "Would that bother you?''

For some silly reason I felt myself blushing. Now, why? He hadn't said, 'If *I* call you Honey or Sugar.' To cover my embarrassment, I began blabbing about how my father used to call me Sparkles. "He said when I was little I was always shooting off sparks of joy. Sickening, isn't it?''

Noel looked down at me. "I think it's a good name. You do have some radiant moments."

I rolled my eyes, as though he'd said something stupid. For a moment I considered asking him if he wanted to come in and meet the quints, but decided against it. I guess I just wanted to keep Noel as someone separate for a while, almost like a secret friend. And I guess, also, I wanted him to go on thinking of me as myself, instead of linking me in his mind with a houseful of babies.

6

The big, final soccer match was coming up in a few days. It was going to be steamy because we'd be playing our archrivals, the team from District 47. Coach Collins called extra practice sessions after school, and we knew, if we wanted to live, we'd better be there for every one of them.

I told Dad about it when we were running the kids through what I called the 'quint wash' that night. I undressed them, Dad dunked them in the tub, and Jean toweled them and put on their sleepers.

"And don't forget," I reminded Dad, "you promised a long time ago that you'd come to the final game."

"Yeh, yeh," Dad muttered, and then almost swore (he was breaking himself of the habit) because Craig had tossed the soap into the toilet bowl.

The next morning, as I was leaving, Dad called out, "Be sure to get home as soon as you can," and assuming he meant 'as soon as you can after practice,' I said I would.

Well! When I did get home—and the coach had kept us later than usual—Dad was there, and was he boiled! "Where were you?" he yelled as I walked in the door.

"Practice," I said. "Why?"

"Why? You're asking me *why?* Do you know," he shouted over the sudden wails of Emma, "I called the school? But they didn't know where you were, either!"

"Dad, there's no mystery. I was right out there on the soccer field! And I told you I had to stay for practice. Last night, when we were bathing the kids. Don't you remember?"

"No, I don't. I didn't hear you. If I had, I'd have said something." He put Emma down. She started to wail again. I picked her up.

"Didn't you know Toots had a late, emergency dental appointment?" Dad went on.

"No."

"Well, she did. And when you didn't show up, I had to rush home again to take over. Natalie, I can't just pick up and leave the office whenever I feel like it. My job's at stake."

"I'm sorry." I was sorry about the mix-up, but I really didn't think it was my fault if Dad couldn't listen and bathe a baby at the same time.

The next morning as we were finishing breakfast, the phone rang. I grabbed it. It was Toots.

"Oh, kiddo, I'm glad I caught you before you left," she said. "I'm going to have to fade out of there early again today. All that dentist did yesterday was take X rays and read the riot act to me about eating hard candies. He said I had one cavity the size of the Grand

43

Canyon and he's going to fill it today. My tooth, I mean. Not the Grand Canyon.''

"Right," I said. "Do you want to talk to Jean?" I handed over the phone and edged toward the door. Dad pinned me with a look.

When Jean hung up, she said, "Oh, darn. Aunt Thelma has to leave early again today and I don't know . . ." She frowned. "We're really swamped at the office. Several people are out with the flu."

"Don't look at me," Dad said. "I have a budget session I can't get out of. Natalie, it looks like . . ."

"Oh, Jack," Jean said, "it isn't fair to ask Natalie." She clicked her fingernail against her teeth, something she did when she was worried and uncertain. "It's not her problem."

"It wasn't her problem yesterday, either," Dad said. Boy, could he hold a grudge.

Sullenly I said, "Yesterday wasn't my fault. I told you I'd be late. I can't help it if you forgot."

"Why is it, Natalie," he said, "that soccer means more to you than your family? You know we're in a bind. Is it such a sacrifice, for once in your life, to give up—"

Jean broke in. "Jack, it really *isn't* Natalie's problem. I don't see why you always—"

Angrily, Dad broke in. "And I don't see why you always take *her* side. According to you—"

"Oh, forget it!" I shouted, sweeping my books off the counter. "I'll come home early if that's what you want. Boy, you sure can tell who rates around here!" I stomped out and slammed the door behind me. Now Dad and Jean were probably yelling at each other, but what did I care?

44

I raged with fury for a couple of blocks but then suddenly fear, cold fear, took its place. Today's practice was only the most crucial of the soccer season, and Collins wasn't about to let me or anyone else out of it. Not for any little they-need-me-at-home kind of reason. I'd have to come up with a better excuse than that.

All morning long I thought of one alibi after another. None sounded convincing. Finally, at noon, I asked Choo Choo and Jiggs if they could come up with a surefire suggestion.

"Just don't tell him the truth," Jiggs advised. "Collins would chew you up and spit you out if you came up with a weak excuse like baby-sitting." My thoughts exactly.

"Dear Jiggs, your language is so graphic," Choo Choo said, sounding above it all. "I think you should tell the coach that you have symptoms of a dread disease, and you think too much of your teammates to expose them to the virus."

"Be serious," Jiggs said. "We don't want to put Natalie here in quarantine. We only want to get her out of practice for one day. Besides, if she had some kind of bug, Coach would just round up a surgical mask for her, or something."

Choo Choo sighed wearily. "Then it's up to you. I gave you my best."

Jiggs looked thoughtful. "You know, I once heard of a guy who wanted to keep out of the army, so he shot off his toe."

Choo Choo and I stared at her, shocked and disgusted.

Jiggs shrugged. "It was just a thought."

*   *   *

After mulling the problem over most of the afternoon I decided to go with the germ approach, only without heroics. I'd simply say I felt rotten and had to go home.

The weird thing is, as the day wore on, I actually did feel as though I were running a fever. And I sneezed, without trying to, twice. I did it when I was talking to the coach. He backed away and told me to go home and to bed, get plenty of rest and drink lots of orange juice, and be set tomorrow for the last big practice before the game. I promised I would.

Toots was all ready to leave when I walked in the door. "I just hope my appointment today is the end of it, and I can kiss that dentist good-bye," she said. "Kiss! That's just a figure of speech, kid, so don't get ideas about me and the dentist!" She started out, but turned. "In case you're wondering why it's so quiet around here, I think those babies are coming down with something. They never sleep this much as a rule."

She was right. Three of the quints seemed feverish and when they did get up they didn't tear around as usual. They all wanted to be held. I wondered if their throats felt scratchy, the way mine did.

Jean called the pediatrician that night and Dad went out to the pharmacy for medicine. They went to bed early, and so did I.

The next morning Jean called her office to say she wouldn't be in, and then she called and told her aunt not to come over. "There's no use in exposing you, too," she said.

I wanted to tell Jean I'd come home right after school, but if I skipped another practice, I'd be on the coach's hit list. He didn't forget things like that.

I was trying to eat my cereal that I'd let get mushy, but it hurt so much to swallow I just gave up. Then, suddenly, tears started streaming down my cheeks. Not the sad kind of tears, the cold-in-the-head kind.

Jean rushed over and put a hand on my forehead. "Honey, you're burning up! Oh, for heaven's sake, you've caught their colds. You poor thing! Now, you go right up to bed, you hear? I'll bring you juice and aspirin and—"

"No, I've got to go."

In a nice but stern voice, Jean said, "Natalie . . . to bed!"

I didn't argue. I was feeling worse by the minute. This was probably my punishment for . . . for . . . I was too tired and weepy-feverish to care what for.

I slept all day. Later on, I thought of the team out on the practice field. And then I rolled over and slept some more.

7

○■○■○

I didn't know if I should show up for the game on Saturday or not. If I didn't, and coach found out I wasn't dead, he'd kill me. If I did show up, he'd probably shoot me on sight.

On Friday night, I phoned Jiggs. "What do you think I should do? Ship out on the next boat or just show up? How ticked is Coach Collins?"

"I don't think he's ticked at all. I heard him say, 'Too bad Wentworth's in sick bay,' something like that."

"*Something like that.* Did he say I was off the team?"

"I don't think so."

"Oh, Jiggs." She was no help at all. "It's important, you know, whether I get to play or not. My dad is actually going to the game. I think he wants to make some things up to me. Anyway, he'll be there, so I'd better be playing. You have no idea, though?"

"Hey, give me a break. I can't read the coach's mind, such as it is. Oh . . . have you heard the news?"

48

"What news?"

"I guess you haven't. She'll call and tell you."

"Who?"

"Michelle."

"What?"

"I just said she'll call and tell you." In her usual abrupt way, Jiggs then said, "Gotta go," and hung up.

I lay on my stomach on the bed, arms crisscrossed under my chin. What could Michelle have to say? It was crazy, but could it be something about Noel? And her? But what—going steady? I didn't think her mother would let her.

I jumped when the phone rang, right next to my elbow. My hand reached out instantly, but I made myself wait for the second ring. I'd read somewhere that you should never answer a phone on the first ring . . . the guy might think you were there by the phone, waiting for his call. Even if you were, you shouldn't let him know it. Not many boys called me, but I was training myself to get into the second-ring habit.

"Hello," I said, trying to sound interested but not anxious, another of the hints.

"Hi! It's Michelle."

"Michelle! What's been going on?"

"Nothing much."

"Too bad, I was out of school. Thought I might have missed some high excitement, like a fire drill."

Michelle laughed. "I can see why Noel thinks you're so witty and charming."

I caught my breath. "He thinks that?"

"Yes. Like I do."

"Oh." So, I wondered, did he think I was witty and charming and say so, or did he simply agree with

49

Michelle when she said it? I couldn't ask. "How is he
. . . Noel?"

"All right. I guess he's coming over, too. It was
supposed to be a surprise, but I found out, so it won't
be a surprise, just a party."

A party. I was relieved that's all it was, and then I
was glad that's what it was. There weren't many
parties around these days. "Is it someone's birthday?" And then I remembered. Oh, wow. It was *hers.*
"Just kidding, Michelle," I said. "When's the party?"

"Tomorrow night. That's when my birthday is.
Well, all day tomorrow's my birthday, of course,
but—"

"Isn't this rather sudden? Not your birthday, the
party."

"Yes, well, it is, but my mother has been so busy
lately, taking Nicole to model interviews and everything."

"Oh, your sister." Nicole was as pretty as Michelle,
but younger. That mother of theirs certainly had an
eye for business. "Who else is coming to the party?"

"Jiggs is for sure." I could almost see Michelle
wrinkling her pretty forehead. "So far we haven't been
able to reach Choo Choo. She's out of town for a
great-uncle's funeral, or maybe an aunt's. I hope she'll
feel like a party, if she gets back in time."

"Oh, she will. What time should we be there?"

Not too early, I hoped. I'd need time to remove the
sweat and grime from the soccer match, provided I
got to play at all, and make a special effort to look
smasheroo for Michelle's party. Where Noel might be.

"It's like . . . I guess . . . eight o'clock? You'll be
here?"

50

"I wouldn't miss it for the world!"

We hung up and I let my head and arms dangle over the side of the bed, just knocked out about the idea of it. A party! And wow, tomorrow night! Things were warming up in my life.

Just as I was about to go down and tell Dad about the invitation, he came upstairs to what had been their bedroom but was now the TV room. "Want to join me?"

Actually, the airport drama he watched every week was a total bore, but maybe I'd be able to ask him about the party during one of the commercials. He ought to be glad, really, that I had this chance to have some fun for a change.

I flopped on the sofa beside him. "What's Jean doing?"

"Talking to her mother. Another fifty-dollar phone bill."

I could tell Dad didn't mean that. Jean's mother lived in New York State and they often visited by phone, but not to the tune of fifty dollars.

I looked at the show, but I wasn't really paying attention. My mind was on the party . . . who'd be there and what we'd do.

When a woman came on with the earth-shaking news that she had switched to a new oven cleaner, I turned down the sound. "Dad, could you drive me to a party tomorrow night?" I thought that was a better way to approach him than an *Is it okay if I go?*

"What party is that?" he asked.

"Michelle's."

"Oh, pretty little Michelle." Dad thought she was a doll, and so quiet, too. He liked Jiggs and Choo Choo

51

too, but instead of dolls, he called them the Comedy Team. "Where is the party?"

"At Michelle's house."

"Her parents going to be home?"

"Of course." I was pretty sure they would be.

"All right. If you feel up to it." The show came back on. "Oh, no," Dad groaned, as the pilot seemed to lose control of the plane. "What a klutz!"

At the next break, I said to Dad, "What did you mean, if I feel up to it? If I feel well enough to play in the game tomorrow afternoon, I'll for sure be up to a little party."

"You're playing on a Saturday?"

"Dad! It's the big game! Don't tell me you forgot! You said you were coming to it, nothing could keep you from it. Remember?"

"Oh. Right. I forgot. But I ought to stick around here and give Jean a hand. Watch the quints while she does the laundry." He put his arm around my shoulder. "Some other time, maybe."

I jerked away. A pair of hot tears spilled down my cheeks. I wanted to say, *The quints always come first with you, don't they?* but instead, I just got up and started out of the room.

Dad turned his head. "Where are you going? Don't you want to see how this thing ends?"

"No." I left.

I took out my soft lenses and then stood under the shower, crying, for a long time. I just didn't count anymore.

My phone rang once, but I didn't feel like talking to anyone. Sometime later, I lay in my darkened room, listening to Pink Floyd. I was almost asleep when my door opened, and Dad said, "Natalie?"

"What."

"Jean's arranged for her friend Sally to come over tomorrow and help out. So I'll be able to go to your game after all."

I didn't say anything for a minute. Then I mumbled, "All right."

He stood hesitating, but when I didn't say anything else, he left. I guess he'd expected a bigger response from me. But why should I be all that grateful for something he'd promised to do in the first place?

The coach was in a surprisingly good mood the next day, probably because Ms. Bredlow was beaming her smile his way. He let me play through most of the game, taking me out now and then to store up energy for the last glorious moments. We won easily.

Dad came down from the bleachers to congratulate us.

Choo Choo, who had something of a crush on my dad, said, "Oh, I think it's just marvelous, Mr. Went-worth, that you take such an interest in Natalie's activities. I only hope my father will give me that kind of support when I tread the boards."

Dad, who hadn't a clue what she was talking about, just smiled and said, "Uh-huh. I'm sure he will."

Later, in the locker room, Choo Choo and Jiggs and I got over in a corner together and talked about the party.

"Listen, I know less than you little innocents about what's going on," Choo Choo said. "I've been away, remember. It was so sad, even though I hardly knew

53

Great Uncle Ned. So tell me, who's invited to the party?''

"Didn't ask," Jiggs said. "Who cares, as long as Trish isn't one of them?"

"It matters a lot," Choo Choo said, whipping out her lipstick. "I don't know about you two, but I'm going to dress as though it's a real evening."

"With boys, you mean?" Jiggs stood waiting.

"Absolutely. What are you wearing, Natalie?"

"The same old thing, probably. The blue."

"Well, then try to do something exciting with your hair," Choo Choo advised.

I pulled it up, twisted it, and held it straight up. "Like this?"

"Oh, ravishing." Choo Choo finished her lipsticking and we all left. Her mother was waiting in the car to take us on a fast gift-buying trip. I ended up getting Michelle a cute pair of earrings in the shape of little red arrows. So far Michelle was the only one of us who had pierced ears. Her mother had had them done for her when she was eleven, for a shampoo ad.

That evening Jiggs' father, wearing his usual workout clothes, drove us to the party. "You guys act like little ladies tonight," he said as we got out of the car. "Don't get into any wrestling matches."

"Come on, Pop," Jiggs said. "We're beyond that kid stuff."

"Yeh, I guess you're more into kissing games now, eh?" He laughed. "If you play post office, watch out for those special deliveries."

"Oh, sick," Jiggs muttered.

As we walked toward the house, Choo Choo said, "Your father has a bizarre sense of humor."

"Yeh. Weird City."

I had a shaky feeling. What if there *were* guys there—Noel and others—and what if? But kids didn't play those games anymore, did they? If so, I certainly hadn't heard of it.

Another car drove up just as we got to the door, and Shannon and Kristen got out. And then just behind them, another car pulled up.

Choo Choo waited to ring the doorbell, to see who else was coming. "Oh, Natalie—woooo!" she said. "It's Troy and Jerry. Troy will be so thrilled to be in the same room with you!"

"Is that still going on?" Jiggs asked.

"No, it's not. And it never was," I said. "Claudia, would you just ring the bell?"

She didn't, though. She waited until the guys joined us. Jerry, with his idiotic grin and his hair plastered flat on his head, and his face full of zits, was as revolting as ever. I had the feeling that Troy hung out with him because the contrast made him look even better. Sure, Troy was good-looking, but I'd realized, after weeks of trying to talk to him, that looks didn't mean all that much. I reached over and punched the doorbell.

Michelle's mom opened the door. "Oh, wonderful to see you!" she exclaimed in a high-pitched, party kind of voice.

Michelle drifted out into the hall. She seemed pleased but a little overwhelmed. She looked prettier than ever, in a sweater and skirt the same violet shade as her eyes.

We were ushered into the living room. Noel was there. Was his smile especially for me, or was it just a smile left over from looking at Michelle? Then I noticed a man and woman who were probably his parents.

Ignoring the other kids for the moment, Michelle's mother put an arm around me and pulled me forward. "This is the little girl I was telling you about," she said, beaming. "The one with quintuplets in the family."

I could have died.

"How exciting," Noel's father murmured. "How lucky you are!"

"Yes, indeed," Mrs. Lawrence said. "And I understand, Natalie, that you live just down the street from us. Sometime, if it's possible, we'd surely enjoy meeting the little celebrities." Her voice was accented, but the words came out strong and clear.

"Uh . . . folks . . ." Noel said.

"Oh, now," his father said, "your mother would never barge in." He smiled at me. "It must be hectic, having five little ones in the house."

"But Natalie doesn't mind, do you, dear?" Michelle's mom said. "She's a regular little mother's helper," she explained to one and all. I don't know where she got her facts. She'd never been in our house.

Choo Choo, whether to come to my rescue or just to direct attention to her own little self, stepped forward then and said, "I'm Claudia Traine." She shook hands with Noel's parents. "Informally known as Choo Choo." To make it clear, she added, "Choo Choo Traine."

"Oh, yes. Of course." They didn't seem to know whether this was meant to be humorous or not.

"And this is Jiggs, Jennifer Farrell."

"Hiya," Jiggs said, and shook hands. From the way Mr. Lawrence winced, she must have given him her bone-crusher grip.

By then Michelle's father had come into the room, carrying drinks for the adults. After the rest of the introductions, we were allowed to go off to the TV room.

Noel appeared next to me. "Sorry about all that," he murmured.

"It's okay."

I went into the room with the others and tried to smile and act as though everything really was okay, but the party had been ruined for me. No one ever said anymore, "Oh, Natalie, you're so nice or so bright," or so whatever. All they ever said now was, "Oh, Natalie, you're the one with quints in the family! How exciting! How wonderful!"

It wasn't wonderful at all. And it wasn't fair. I had a right to be myself . . . Natalie Wentworth. Me. Just me. I was more than just *the sister of the quints!* Wasn't I?

8

○■○■○

We all got Cokes and sat around talking for a while, but the party wasn't really taking off.

"So what's the game plan for tonight?" Jiggs asked in her usual blunt way.

"Game plan?" Michelle looked anxious. "I . . . I don't know."

"Would you like me to do my imitation of Mae West?" Choo Choo volunteered. She got up, and with fingers splayed against her hips, sashayed across the room to Jerry. "Hey-uh, big boy. Whyn't ya come up'n see me sometime?"

It was fairly funny, but not funny enough to make Troy, who was sitting next to me on the sofa, fall sideways, with his head landing on my shoulder. I gave him a shove.

"Hey," he said, raising up. "I can't help falling apart. That Choo Choo just knocks me out."

"Watch it, or I'll knock you out, too," I muttered.

"Anyone for charades?" Choo Choo called out.

No one seemed eager to play, except for Shannon.

58

Michelle looked the worried hostess, not knowing which side to take.

Choo Choo didn't give up easily. "Anyone else have a suggestion? No? All right then, we'll count off. Michelle, you're one and Jiggs is two. Noel one, Kristen two. And so on."

I was glad to be on the team with Michelle, Noel and Shannon. Troy was on the opposite team.

"It's uneven," Jerry complained. "Four and five."

"Makes no difference," Choo Choo said firmly. "Michelle, just trot off and find some paper we can tear into slips, and also locate a couple of ball-points."

"Mind if I go get some more sodas?" Noel asked Michelle. "Before we get into the game?"

"Oh, please do. You know where everything is." Michelle was rummaging through a drawer in a wall unit, looking for supplies.

"Come along and help, Natalie?" Noel asked.

"Sure." I leaped up, glad to get away from Troy.

In the kitchen Noel pulled Cokes and Sprites from the refrigerator. "Is he your boyfriend or what? That Troy guy."

"I can't stand him."

"He seems to like you."

"I can't help that."

"Should we take in the other package of Fritos?"

"I guess. Here, I can carry some of those." I cradled the Fritos and reached for a couple of cans of soda.

"I know how he feels, though. Poor guy." Noel smiled, then started away before I could ask exactly what he meant by that poor guy stuff. Something about me? But . . . why? And then it came to me. He knows how Troy feels because he, Noel, feels that way about Michelle! Was that it? Did he like Michelle a lot, but she didn't want to be alone with him, so she insisted on having lots of kids over? It didn't seem possible. How could anyone not like Noel?

As we went back into the TV room I stopped so suddenly, from shock, that Noel bumped me from behind. I couldn't believe my eyes. Trish was there!

"Oh, hi, you two," she said.

I couldn't utter a word.

Noel said, "Hi" and went back out for another soda.

I looked toward Michelle, but she avoided my eyes. Choo Choo and Jiggs didn't say anything. They didn't have to. Their expressions said it all.

Trish, totally at ease, sat on the sofa next to Troy, so close you couldn't have passed a piece of dental floss between them. He looked a bit rattled for a moment, but then he draped an arm around Trish's shoulder and gave me a smug look.

Was I supposed to be jealous or what? I wasn't, but I probably looked as though I was. I flopped down on a hassock across the room.

Choo Choo broke the awkward silence. "At least now we have an even number for the teams," she said. "Trish, you're with Michelle, Noel, Natalie and Shannon, so get over on the other side of the room."

"I happen to like it here," Trish said, giving Troy a sickening smile. He squeezed her shoulder. It was a truly revolting sight.

Kristen got up. "I'll go on the other team," she said. She joined her friend Shannon. Choo Choo, clearly annoyed that she hadn't broken up the twosome, explained the game. After Michelle passed out the paper and pens, our group went out of the room to think up our titles.

When we were ready to begin, Choo Choo volunteered to go first. She acted out the whole title of the book, in this case, by pretending to whitewash a fence. It didn't take long for our team to guess it was *Tom Sawyer*.

Noel volunteered to start off for our team. He stood there, wild-eyed, gasping, and flapping his arms, trying to act out the movie title. We yelled everything from *Return of Godzilla* to *The Swamp Creature*, but no one ever did guess he was doing *The Poseidon Adventure*.

Michelle's title, *Revenge of the Nerds*, was almost impossible to act out, at least for her. She stood there looking hopeless, until her time was up. I felt sorry for her.

Mine, *Catcher in the Rye*, wasn't too bad. I let my team know it was four words, and the last word sounded like *eye*. They yelled out, *bye, cry, die* and so on, and when they finally got to *rye*, it was simple. I felt stupid, though, because of the way Trish kept looking at me and then whispering to Troy and making him laugh.

When Trish herself got up, she tried to be cute and flirty. Then Troy, for his turn, did a lot of stupid things that had Trish and Jerry in hysterics, but which weren't all that funny to the rest of us.

Once everyone had had a turn, the game was over, and no one wanted to play another round. The party really died then.

After listening to silly, aimless talk for a while, I

went over to Michelle and asked if I could go to her room and use the phone. She said, "Of course," and I motioned for her to come along with me.

Once we got inside her door, I said, "How come you invited Trish?"

"I didn't," Michelle said.

"What?"

"She invited herself. She called late this afternoon and told me she was sorry that no one at home had given her the message about the party, but she could make it, and what time did it start?"

I stared at Michelle. "I just can't believe that even Trish would be that nervy. Well, yes, I guess I can."

Michelle brushed back her hair. "I couldn't tell her I'd never invited her. And now I know why she was so anxious to be in on it. Because of Troy."

"How come you invited *him?*"

"I couldn't have Noel and no other guys. Troy and Jerry were the only ones I could think of to ask. Troy wanted to know if you'd be here. Natalie, I have the feeling that he still likes you."

"Sure, I believe that. The way he's carrying on with Trish."

"Oh, but can't you tell? It's just to make you jealous." Michelle looked earnest. "I really believe that."

"Yeh, well, I can hardly stand to be in the same room with him."

"I'm sorry for inviting him, then. There's the phone."

"I don't really need to call anyone. It was just an excuse to . . ." I glanced around her room then, and gasped at what I saw. "Michelle? Your room—it's so different. What happened?"

"It was a birthday present from my parents."

"Wow. Did you pick out everything yourself?" It didn't have a Michelle kind of look. Everything was so bold and brassy now.

"No, I didn't know anything about it. I came home from school and it was all changed. It's different, isn't it?" She said all this in a sad kind of voice.

It certainly was different. Instead of the pink ruffled and dotted Swiss softness of before, there was now a pop art, trendy look. Lots of black, with red and yellow patterns. Even the old, plump pillows had been replaced with hard-looking stiff ones. Most of all, though, the things Michelle had loved so much, her stuffed animals and the big doll her grandmother had given her when she was little, were gone.

"Where's Lovey-Baby?" I asked. Michelle used to hold the doll whenever she was in the room. She was really attached to it.

"Put away." Michelle blinked. "I'm too old for dolls."

"Oh." Her mother's idea, I could tell. "Well . . ." I didn't know what to say. "I guess we'd better go back to the others."

We did. After that it wasn't very long until we joined the adults for birthday cake and ice cream and then the party broke up. Jiggs' father came and got us. "Kind of early, isn't it?" he asked.

"We were all tired and dragged out," Jiggs said, "after the big game this afternoon."

"Kids." Her father shook his head. "No stamina these days. It must be all that junk food you eat."

Most of the others had left about the same time we did. All except Noel and his parents. I wondered, on the ride home, if by now Noel and Michelle had gone back to the TV room. If so, were they sitting close together, the way Trish and Troy had done? I couldn't picture it.

To make myself forget all that, I asked the girls what they thought of the new decorating job in Michelle's room. They'd been in there after I was.

"Spiffy," Jiggs said.

Choo Choo disagreed. "It's awful. It looks like the teen section of some department store. I'm really surprised that Michelle would choose stuff like that."

"She didn't," I told her. "Her mother did. It was a birthday gift, all done when Michelle was at school."

"That explains it." In an unusually somber tone, Choo Choo went on, "Mothers shouldn't do things like that without asking a kid's opinion. Your own room should be private and the way you want it to be."

"Oh, well," Jiggs said, "at least she got rid of those dumb stuffed animals and especially that life-size doll. Boy, talk about immature!"

"Maybe Michelle needs to hold on to something childish," I said. "Her mom tries to make her grow up so fast."

"Speaking of childish," Choo Choo said, "how about the way Trish and Troy acted this evening? Didn't it make you want to gag?"

"Yes," I said, "but did you find out how Trish happened to be there? That'll really make you retch."

They hadn't heard, so I told them. Sure enough, Choo Choo and Jiggs made such loud gagging sounds that Jiggs' father threatened to throw us all out of the car. He was kidding, though.

Choo Choo, settling down, said, "Trish has a lot of gall, but even so, I almost have to feel sorry for her."

"For Trish?" I gasped. "You must be out of your mind."

"Listen, she'd do anything, *anything* to impress Troy. And she doesn't realize he's just using her."

"How is he using her?"

"To make you jealous. Natalie, anyone can see that Troy is still mad for you."

"Oh, please."

"It's true. So if you want him back . . ."

"Would you cut it out?" I wondered what Jiggs' father was thinking, hearing all of this. Mostly for his benefit, I said, "We're too young to be all that interested in boys anyway."

"That's the ticket," Jiggs' dad said, looking at us in the rearview mirror. "You tell 'em, Nat-baby."

I wondered what he and the girls would have to say if they knew how interested I was in Noel. The truth was, I thought about him a lot. A whole big lot. For all the good it did me.

9

I hate Sunday morning breakfasts. We always eat late and with the quints. Before they were born, when there were just the three of us, we'd have waffles or pancakes with blueberries, or great omelettes that were jazzed up in some special way.

Now, though, it was almost impossible to make omelettes and keep them warm enough to eat, considering the quints and their constant demands. We couldn't have pancakes because Jean didn't want the quints to eat heavy foods, and they'd raise a ruckus if they saw us eating something they couldn't have. So now we stuck to ordinary stuff.

The morning after the party, Jean asked if it had been fun. She was holding Craig's hands to keep him from throwing scrambled eggs at his neighbors. "Did you play games or what?"

"One game. Michelle didn't even open her gifts. I guess because not everyone brought one. Oh, but the biggest gift was from her parents, anyway. They had her bedroom redone." I glanced at Dad to see if he was impressed. My own birthday was in less than a week and I was hoping for something on the spectacular side, like a big portable radio/tape player.

"Speaking of birthdays," Dad said, "we have a pretty important one coming up ourselves."

I looked down at my plate and smiled. *Important?* I was glad he realized how important it really was.

"In just ten days now," Dad said.

Ten days? He was wrong. It was . . . let's see . . . only six. And then I realized he was talking about the quints!

"Isn't it hard to believe the quints will be one year old?" Dad went on. "It seems like only yesterday."

"Not to me," Jean said. She took Craig out of his high chair and set him on the floor. "If you're going to keep messing around like that, you're finished," she told him.

And then as I sat there, unable to swallow another bite, the two of them, Jean and Dad, began talking about what they were going to do to celebrate the Big One.

"I'd like to have pictures taken," Jean said. "Not just with the old home camera, but real photos. At a studio." Before Dad could mention money, she said, "Honey, I know it'll be expensive and I know we have to start cutting down, but this is special. I mean, it's their first birthday and we ought to have a great record of it."

"I guess," Dad said. "We'd never forgive ourselves someday if we didn't. They'll only be one year old this once. I'll make an appointment."

Jean jumped up and grabbed Craig, who was slamming a cupboard door and barely missing his fingers.

67

"Jack, do you think we should invite some people over, have a cake and everything?"

"Absolutely. It'll make a terrific movie." Dad suddenly seemed to notice my silence and the way I was just sitting there.

"Natalie, let's have your picture taken, too," he said with a touch of guilt in his tone. "I'll bet your mother would love to have a new one."

I didn't dare say anything for fear I would burst out crying. Not one word about *my* birthday. He'd forgotten it altogether.

"Do you have to sit there with a scowl on your face?" Dad said after a moment. "If you don't want to be photographed, just say so. No one is going to force you."

"Forget it!" I almost wailed, and ran from the room.

"What in the . . ." I heard Dad say. And then I heard Jean's "Oh no! Oh Jack!"

I couldn't hear anything else because I was dashing up the stairs. Just as I got to my room, I heard Dad down below call out, "Honey!"

I slammed the door and fell onto the bed. This is what it had come to. The most important day in any kid's life was the day she'd been born. And now my birthday meant nothing as far as Dad was concerned. All because of the five little darlings who ruled the whole house. Well, they could rule it without me. I was leaving! I really was. Mother would be burned when I told her how I rated around here. She'd insist that I come out to Colorado immediately.

There was a knock on my door, and Jean said softly, "Natalie, may I come in?"

68

I wanted to shout, "No! Stay with your husband and the brats!" but I didn't blame Jean. She wasn't my parent.

She opened the door slightly and peeked in. "Could I talk to you for a minute, Natalie?"

I didn't answer.

She came in and sat on the edge of the bed. "I can't tell you how sorry I am, Natalie . . . how sorry we both are. It was unforgivable of us to have carried on that way about the babies, when you . . . when your birthday is coming up in just a few days. I don't know what to say."

I lay there on my stomach, my face turned away from her. I couldn't see the expression on her face, but I could guess how she looked.

"It must seem to you," she went on, "that the quints always take first place. But it's only because they're still so little and need so much care. I wish it weren't that way. I remember the good times we used to have, you and your dad and I. But we'll just have to wait until the quints get bigger and aren't so much bother, and then maybe we can have some fun times again."

We'll never have days like that again, I thought. How could we? They'll always be around, unless someone kidnaps them, and who'd be stupid enough to do a thing like that?

Jean talked on for a while and then asked if I had any plans for the evening.

I turned toward her. "No. Why?"

"Well, we were going to take the quints to the forest preserve, let them run around, use up some of their energy. They ought to conk out early this evening, and I was wondering if the three of us could take in a movie. We could even eat out. What a treat, huh?''

"I don't know." I didn't see why I should let Dad get off so easily. How could a father forget his first-born's birthday?

"Jean!" Dad called from downstairs. "We'd better get moving. They're tearing up the joint."

"Men," Jean said with a smile. "They just can't cope."

"They don't want to. It's easier to have someone else do their dirty work." I got up and went to my desk. "I guess I'll finish up my homework."

"Good idea," Jean said, getting up, too. "Clear the decks for tonight." She paused at the door. "If you want to go."

"Yeh. We'll see."

Dad was yelling up the stairs again, and Jean, on her way, called, "All right, all right, keep your shirt on."

As soon as she was gone, I flopped back on the bed. I heard the sounds from downstairs as they chased the kids and got them into whatever they were wearing. Then there was the commotion of getting them all into the car. Lately, Dad had been talking about getting a van. I'd wanted, from the time I was little, for him to get a camper, but he'd always said Mom wasn't the rugged outdoor type, and it wouldn't be fun for just the two of us. Well, that was no problem now!

I lay there waiting. Waiting for them to get going. And then I was going to get going myself. Right to the phone. I'd make that call to Mother and arrange to go out to Colorado as soon as possible . . . maybe even in time for my birthday. That would be my gift to myself—freedom. Freedom from this houseful of quints, and from Dad.

With trembling fingers, I dialed Mom's number. The phone rang and rang. She didn't answer.

10

○■○■○

We didn't go to the movies that night after all. Dad got bitten by a wasp at the forest preserve, right above his left eye. His lid was swollen almost shut by the time they got home. I didn't think he looked ready for a M*A*S*H unit or anything, but Jean fussed around, putting on ointment and even a bandage around his head, covering the eye.

"You girls go to the flicks without me," Dad said later. "I'll be all right. Don't worry about me."

Jean looked dubious.

"You'd better stay here and nurse the invalid," I told her. "We can go some other tme."

I was glad to get out of going with them anyway. I still hadn't forgiven Dad and probably wouldn't for a long time, if ever. The fact that Mom hadn't answered the phone this afternoon just made me put my hurt on hold. Until I did reach her, I wasn't going to let Dad smooth things over and soften my feelings. He'd really done it this time, and I wasn't going to forgive and forget. He'd be sorry when he found out he was losing me for good.

The next morning started out like every other Monday morning, except that we were going to get still another sitter. The Queen of the Cookie Jar had resigned for good, and late last night Jean had finally reached a woman on a list someone had given her. This one's name was Mrs. Winkleman, and she promised to check in by eight the next morning.

But now it was almost time for all of us to leave and she hadn't shown up yet. Dad looked at his watch. "I'll give her five minutes more."

And then what? I wondered.

At that moment the phone rang. Jean groaned. "Oh, no! She's not backing out on us!" She picked up the phone, looked puzzled, then said, "Oh, I don't know about that. Just a minute." She turned to Dad. "It's the local paper. They want to take pictures of the quints."

"Absolutely not!" he roared, loud enough for the person on the phone to hear.

"I'm afraid we'd rather not," Jean said into the phone. But the person must have been rather persuasive because after a bit Jean said, "Here, I'll let you talk to my husband."

Dad looked disgusted, but took the phone and said, "I'm Jack Wentworth, father of the quints, and we prefer not to have their pictures in the paper, okay?" He listened, then said, "Yes, I know it's their first birthday, but it's not world-class news. We intend to keep the celebration within the family."

Just then Mrs. Winkleman arrived, apologizing for

having to stop and get gas on the way. She looked like an ordinary middle-aged woman, with a lot of gray in her short hair. She'd turn totally gray if she hung around the quints for long.

Jean took the sitter into the nursery to show her the little darlings. Dad was still arguing on the phone, but he seemed to be losing steam. He was saying, "I realize that," or "Maybe so, but . . ." Then he said, "Just a minute," put his hand on the phone and said to me, "Go get your mother."

"Who?"

"Jean . . . Jean. Go get her."

I'd been about to leave. I dropped my stuff on the table and went to the quints' room, where Jean was showing the sitter around. "Dad wants you."

When we got back to the kitchen, Dad said to Jean, "They've offered to take portraits along with some informal shots. What do you think? It would save all that hassle of taking the babies to the photographer's."

"Oh, Jack, I'd really like . . ."

"So what shall I tell them, yes or no?"

"I don't know." Jean looked at the clock. "Oh well, all right."

Dad told the guy on the phone that it was okay, but to call back that night to set up the time because he was already late for work. After he'd hung up, Dad said to Jean, "They're not going to give up. Even if we didn't let them come around they'd find some way of sneaking pictures. You know how persistent these news hounds can be."

We all did. The papers, magazines and TV crews had nearly driven us crazy when the quints were born, and for weeks afterward. And now they were starting in again.

"It'll just be this once," Dad said, as he followed Jean on her way to give Mrs. Winkleman more instructions. "And at least we'll get some good pictures out of the deal."

I grabbed my books and purse and headed for school. They could have every newspaper in the country come in for pictures as far as I was concerned. By the time of the quints' birthday, I'd be off in Colorado. All I had to do was reach Mother and tell her to expect me and I'd be on my way. I'd make the call as soon as I got home.

On my return Mrs. Winkleman met me at the door. "Oh, honey, I'm so glad to see you," she said. "You're the little girl, aren't you?"

"I'm Natalie."

"Yes. We didn't have a chance to meet this morning. Oh, dear!" She looked quite distressed.

"Did they drive you crazy?" I asked.

"Yes, they did. Oh, not the quints! They were angels. It's the calls. I didn't know what to say."

"What calls are you talking about?" I kept my voice low so the "angels" wouldn't hear.

"The papers called, and the TV. They all wanted to know *when,* and I didn't know what to tell them. They called all day. All day long."

"Don't worry. You did the right thing. My dad will handle the press." I tried to sneak by the quints' room but Craig spotted me and they all set up a howl. "Lee! Lee!" Their version of Natalie.

I was eager to get upstairs and make that call to

75

Mom, but then I realized she was an hour behind us and wouldn't be home from class yet anyway. I opened the gate and the quints rushed me like a herd of elephants.

"Oh, my, how they love big sister!" Mrs. Winkleman exclaimed, while the gang nearly pulverized me. And then she said, in a lowered tone, as though the quints shouldn't hear, "Would you mind if I just slipped into the bathroom for a minute?"

I nodded, wondering if she had held off all day. I hoped she wouldn't let the quints totally run the show or she'd burn out before the week was over, and then what would we do?

Upstairs, I sat cross-legged in my big chair and reached for the headphones. I listened to Whitney Houston's latest and then changed tapes, but instead of listening, my mind drifted to last summer.

I remembered the happy times I'd had with Mother in Colorado. It wasn't as though we did anything spectacular, other than taking drives into the mountains, and once, staying overnight at a big park hotel. The happiness came mostly from just being together, and not having any pressures.

One day, when we were driving along, laughing about the time I'd dressed a kitten in doll clothes and it had run up the neighbor's tree, I suddenly said, "Mother, did anyone ever call you Bubbles?"

"Bubbles?" she glanced at me and smiled. "No. Should they?"

"I don't know. Dad used to call me Sparkles."

"I remember."

"But you're more . . . airy . . . and light . . . and iridescent. At least you are right now."

"If I am, it's because you're here." There were little pink splashes of pleasure on her cheeks. "A lot of my friends wanted to meet you, but I'm selfish. I want to keep you all to myself. We have so little time."

"I know."

She let a few minutes pass and then she said, "You could decide to stay, you know."

"Stay? For how long?" I didn't think Dad would like my being away for another week.

"For good." She gave me a look. "We could have your things shipped out. Enroll you in school here."

My day suddenly darkened. "I couldn't do that."

This time Mother stared straight ahead at the road. "Why not?"

"Because . . . well, just because I can't. Maybe I could later on."

"Later on," Mother said sadly. "Then it will be high school, and you'll get all involved with activities and maybe even . . ."

She didn't continue. I had the feeling she'd been about to say "boys," but thought better of it.

"I'd like to live with you, Mother. I miss you a lot."

"But?"

How could I tell her I was afraid of moving all the way to Colorado Springs, and of changing my life completely? And leaving my friends? Besides, Jean and Dad depended on me, and the quints—well, I'd even miss them. To Mom I said, "This just isn't home."

Mother didn't say anything for a bit. Then she

murmured, "Home is what you make of a place. It doesn't have to be where you were born."

"I know, but . . ."

Mother didn't coax. She wasn't the type. I knew she felt sad, though, and so did I. We put up a pretense during my last days there and were still trying to act casual when Mother put me on the plane. I knew she'd cry as soon as I left, though. I cried a little, too, at the take-off, but then I made myself think of how great it would be to get back home. I was only thinking of the good things. The bad things popped up almost as soon as I landed.

When Dad picked me up at the airport, he asked if I'd had a good time. But almost immediately he began complaining about the new sitter, and about how tough it was for him and Jean to be gone all day and then come home to chaos.

"Maybe Jean could quit her job," I said.

"Wonderful," he said. "And how are we supposed to pay all the bills? I hear guys complaining about the expense of one new baby. They should just try keeping up with five of them."

I felt resentful. Here I was, back for fifteen minutes, and he was unloading on me. "You didn't even ask about Mother," I grumbled.

"Oh. Well, how is she?"

"She's fine. We really did have a good time."

"I'm glad. And now, maybe for a couple of weeks before school starts, you can pitch in and help get things stabilized at home."

I felt like telling him it wasn't my job to keep things in order, or to be a little helper around the house, but I didn't want to tangle with Dad. When he was in one of his "down" moods the best thing was to say nothing. Inside I was angry, though. And I was still angry today. Things seemed to be getting worse instead of better. I knew I'd made a huge mistake ever coming back again.

I checked my watch. Too soon to try Mother again. Sighing, I got up, went into the TV room, and flicked on the set.

What would I actually say when I reached Mother? *I've thought it over and decided I want to be with you more than anything in the world.* Hogwash. Mother wouldn't buy that at all. She wasn't naive. *Dad has become a real grouch and the quints are turning into little monsters.* Too whiny. *I want to live in Colorado.* False. False.

I've thought it over and I really feel, in the long run, I'd be happier there. That sounded all right. It was even true.

But what would come next, after I told her I'd be happier there? Would Mother agree that I should come out right away, or would it take a little convincing? She might want some kind of assurance that I had thought this out, and wasn't just calling out of a whim or discontent of the moment.

Mother has a *thing* about my changeable nature, as she calls it. It all dates back to the time when I went to camp, and called that night to tell her I was miserable and wanted to come home. I begged and begged, until she agreed to drive up and get me the next day. But the next morning I called and told her I loved camp now and to please send a lot of bubble gum. *I was only ten years old at the time!* But to this day she declares I have a changeable nature.

If I called now and said I'd changed my mind, she might not take me seriously. So what could I say, what could I do, to convince her?

I stared at the images on the TV screen, without really seeing or hearing. And the words of an old song suddenly filtered through my mind. "You've got to . . . accentuate the positive . . . eliminate the negative . . ." Why? Why did that song come to me?

And then I thought, *It's right.* I shouldn't even mention all the negative things about my life here. Instead, I should think of some positive thing about living with Mom. *Mais oui.* French! *Mais oui* was French for "But yes!" And, yes, French might just be the weapon I could use to make Mom accept my change of plan!

For years and years, Mother had been after me to please learn the language. And for years I had refused. Why? I suppose it was because Mom taught French, and most kids want to distance themselves from anything that interests their parents.

So now I could take the positive approach and say something like, "And Mom, once I get settled in, why don't we start talking French around the house? I might not understand everything you say right at first, but I'll bet I'd catch on pretty fast."

Oh, wow, was I brilliant or what?

Carefully I thought over the plan. There were no flaws in it that I could see. I'd start out by telling Mom I missed her and that I'd made a mistake coming back, and then I'd casually go on to our life out there together and how we could start the French lessons right away. When I reached that point Mom would probably bring up all those things she used to talk about, like how we could go to Paris someday if I learned the language. Now, instead of brushing her off, I'd agree that Paris was a place I really wanted to visit.

So there I'd be, living happily with Mom and picking up the language she loved with not much effort on my part. We'd both be pleased.

I raced back to my room and dialed Mother's number. Still no answer.

Oh well, it didn't matter. I'd try later. I might not make it out of here in time for my birthday, but at least I knew I'd be leaving before long; I could go downstairs with a light heart. Little would Dad and Jean know that they were about to see the last of little Natalie.

11

Although no one blamed Mrs. Winkleman for telling all the news people to call back that night, the constant ringing of the phone nearly drove us bananas.

Most of the calls came during dinnertime. We'd noticed before that people who wanted to sell carpeting or other stuff usually rang up then, when they were pretty sure someone would be home.

Jean answered at first, but Dad took over. It finally came down to this: The papers weren't going to do formal photographs after all. They wanted candid shots. Other papers wanted to take pictures, too. Even the news services. The TV people asked to come to the house the day before the quints' birthday, which would be next Tuesday, so they'd have the film all set for the news broadcasts the next day. Dad finally agreed to let one paper take photos, which they'd have to share with the others. The TV people could have an hour on the night before the birthday.

Dad put his plate into the microwave oven to reheat his food. "I wish we hadn't agreed to anything," he said. "It's going to be one big mess, with those characters taking over the place."

"Right," Jean said. "And now we'll have to make time to have the regular photos taken at the studio. You know, the good ones."

"Couldn't we just let those go?" Dad asked.

"Oh, Jack." Jean lifted Beth out of her chair and carried her to the sink, where she lobbed off a big glob of mashed peas from her terry-clothed leg. "Now's the time to do it. The children are going to change so fast."

"All right, all right," Dad said. "But I wonder how much all this is going to cost."

"Well . . . with the clothes . . ." Jean looked worried.

"What clothes?" Dad stared at her.

"For the photos. Honey, they haven't anything decent to wear for dress-up. Nothing really nice."

"What's wrong with what they usually wear?"

Jean rolled her eyes.

"Dad," I butted in. "What they usually wear is stuff friends give us, that their own kids have outgrown. Haven't you *noticed*? And most of that stuff has food stains or drool . . ."

"What about the outfits your mother sent?" Dad asked Jean.

"Honey. That was at least three months ago. Those things are too little now." She glanced at me and then said, "They've outgrown their shoes, too. So we might as well get everything at once."

Dad just shook his head.

To lighten things up, I said, "That'll be some party. Are you going to have five cakes or just one big cake?"

"I don't know," Jean said. She seemed a bit depressed at the way Dad had complained. "I'll worry about that later." She took the bibs off the quints, then lifted them down from their high chairs and let them run wild for a while. It was our usual nightly routine, and I was getting sick of it.

When the dishes were done, and the quints bathed and tucked into bed, I was free to go upstairs. I wondered if Dad groused about plans for *my* birthday, too. And then I wondered if there *were* any plans for my birthday. I'd be lucky, probably, to get a cake from the bakery.

Mom had always made my birthday cake herself, which was an effort, since she wasn't great in the kitchen. One year she had baked an angel food cake, put a Barbie doll in the center of it, and then cut the cake in tiers and iced it to look like ruffles. Another year, she'd made a gingerbread house with all kinds of candy trim. Jiggs still raved about that one. The very last cake Mom had made for me was shaped like a Princess phone. It hadn't turned out too well, but at least she tried to be original.

I wondered what Mother would send me for my birthday. *She* wouldn't forget. The gift might already be in the mail. But wait. If it wasn't, I could tell her when I called to just keep it there. I'd open it at her house as soon as I arrived.

It was eight o'clock. Surely Mom would be home by now. I was feeling a bit nervous when I dialed. I knew she'd be surprised, and maybe a bit rattled, to hear that I planned to come out to Colorado right away. Mom wasn't crazy about being rushed. I'd make her

84

understand, though, that it was vital for me to come as soon as possible, in order to keep my sanity.

Mother picked up the phone on the third ring. She did seem surprised to hear from me, especially on a Monday night. We usually talked some time over a weekend.

The first thing she said was, "Natalie, is something wrong? Are you all right?"

I hesitated. Something was wrong, but not terribly wrong. "I just wanted to talk with you," I said.

"Oh. I see. Well, what about? Is something going on there?"

"Yes, in a way."

I could almost see her puzzled little frown as she waited for me to go on. I took a breath. "Mother, I've been thinking. Ever since I came back from visiting you, things have been up for grabs around here."

"What do you mean by that?"

"Well, Dad changed to an office job."

"I know that. But what's the problem?"

I hesitated. "He's around here every night now. And he's become a big grouch. And Jean's working really hard, and she can't always get home early, and we're always having sitter problems, and the quints . . . well, they're getting really hard to handle. They don't stay put anymore. And they whine and fight a lot."

"Natalie, that's too bad, all of it, but what do you expect me to do about it? Or are you just calling to unload?"

"I'm calling to tell you I've changed my mind. I'd like to come out there and live with you after all."

There was a long pause. I wished we had video

phones so I could see if my mother was smiling or frowning. "Mom?" I prompted.

"Natalie, you've caught me off guard. This is all such a shock."

"I know. But aren't you glad? Glad I changed my mind?"

"I might be if I didn't know you so well, Natalie. You have a great habit of changing your mind. I remember when . . ."

"Mom, if you're going to bring up summer camp and the bubble gum again, just remember that was a long time ago. I was only ten years old!"

"That's not the only time. Remember when—"

"Mom, I've changed! I mean, I'm different now."

"I seem to recall, when you were here—"

"Mom! Don't you *want* me?" I was close to crying.

"It's not a question of *wanting,* darling. It's a question of being practical. When I realized in August I'd still be alone, I worked out a schedule to keep myself occupied. Besides teaching, I'm into night classes, and on weekends I do volunteer work with troubled teenagers."

I'm a troubled teenager, I thought.

She went on. "You're hitting me with this at a very bad time. If you had only decided last August when I asked you . . . but now I'm locked into a heavy schedule. In fact, I'm busier than when we lived together, back in the apartment. You know how lonesome you used to get then, when I had just those few commitments."

"I'm different now," I protested. "I'd love some peace and quiet. You just can't imagine what it's like, living here. It's like being in a zoo where the animals are running loose! And they're not all that toilet-trained, either.''

"I can imagine it all right, and I sympathize, but really, Natalie, I don't see what—"

I became a bit frantic. "Mom!" It was time to throw in the zinger. "If you let me come live with you now, I'll even learn to speak French!"

The one thing I didn't expect her to do was laugh, but she did. "I must say you do seem desperate," she said with a smile still in her voice. "Although that doesn't change anything about your coming here, it does sound like a good idea for the future."

"The future!"

"You know how I used to say I'd like to take you to Paris with me someday. Well, it might be possible soon. And in the meantime, you could be mastering the language and—"

"How am I supposed to do that? You'd have to teach me!"

"Oh, nonsense, Natalie. You have those tapes I got you a long time ago . . . the ones you never even took out of the box. Dust them off and start listening. That isn't too hard a thing to do, now is it?"

Sullenly I said, "It wouldn't be the same as having a person to talk to."

"No, but it'd be a start."

With tears in my voice I said, "I thought you'd be pleased. I thought you'd want me to be with you, like you said last summer."

"I do want you with me, Natalie. A great deal. But I want you to come because . . ."

"Because what?"

She paused. "Oh, well. We'll go into that later. In

the meantime, you've given yourself a great goal. You'll feel good about yourself, Natalie, accomplishing something like that."

Oh, sure I will, I thought. *What I'll feel is good and stupid for letting myself in for it.*

Mother switched topics. "I'll miss seeing you on your birthday. Be sure your father takes pictures."

Of me? I thought. *Since when?*

"Your present is in the mail. I hope you'll like it. Do you have big plans?"

There was no point now in going on about how I was being ignored. Why should she care anyway, out there with her troubled teenagers?

"I guess we'll have a really big party," I said. "A huge cake and all that." What a liar.

"Wonderful. Well, I'll be thinking of you. Have a lovely birthday, darling, and . . . try not to grow up too much before I see you again."

"Okay. 'Bye, Mom."

" 'Bye. Oh . . . Natalie?"

"What?"

"Remember those girls I told you about last summer? I saw them the other day, and they're really eager to meet you, so maybe next time—"

I broke in. "Mom, could we talk about it later? I have to start studying."

"Oh. Well, all right. Good night then, Natalie."

"Good night."

I hung up. And I could almost see the hurt in my mother's eyes, for the way I'd cut her off. But what about the way she'd treated me? Hadn't she . . . ? I felt awful. And I felt sorry. But I couldn't call her back and tell her so. I just couldn't.

Nothing in my life was working out the way it should. I'd thought going to Mother's was the answer, but it hadn't turned out to be. What had Mother meant when she said *"I want you to come because . . ."* I couldn't figure her out. I couldn't figure anything out. I wasn't even sure now what it was I wanted.

Why did life have to be such a problem?

12

○■○■○

Sometimes strange and wonderful things happen in my life. An hour or so after I talked to Mother, my phone rang. I assumed it was Choo Choo, who usually called around that time.

"Hi, you twit," I said. "Talk fast. I'm expecting a call from Prince Edward."

"Oh, rilly," the male voice said, with an English accent. "I thought it was all off between you two."

"Noel?" Oh, wow. Why was he calling? "Is this rilly Noel?" I asked, echoing his accent.

"The same. Can you talk for a few minutes?"

"Sure." I could talk for hours, to him. "What's goin' on?"

"Nothing much. Did you enjoy the party?"

"Of course." I didn't want to say what I really thought, because of his closeness to Michelle. I wondered how close that closeness actually was. "Did you stay long after the rest of us left?" Again, I had that vision of him and Michelle, maybe sitting together on the sofa.

"No, we left right after. I've been wondering what you think about Michelle."

What I think about Michelle? How about what you think about her! "I don't know what you mean," I said.

"She seems so . . . I don't know. Unhappy."

"You mean all the time, or just last Saturday?"

"All the time. Or maybe it's just around me. I don't know." He paused. "Anyway, the main reason I called is . . ."

I waited. What was this wonderful thing he was about to say?

". . . is to tell you I'm sorry my folks embarrassed you that way about the quintuplets."

What a letdown. "That's okay," I mumbled.

"You must get sick of hearing people talk about them. I would."

"Yeh, well, it hasn't been so bad lately. The excitement has more or less died down." Then I added, in a somewhat mournful voice, "But wouldn't you know, with the quints' birthday coming up, it's going to start all over again."

"Why?"

"Why? Because the newspapers are going to take a bunch of pictures. And get this . . . there's even going to be TV coverage!"

I'd expected Noel to sympathize, but he was just like anyone else. "No kidding!" he said. "They'll be on TV? You must be thrilled!"

"Not really," I said. And then to show how truly unaffected I was, I casually asked, "Are you trying out for basketball?"

"Basketball?" He sounded the least bit confused.

"Oh. Well, I was planning on trying out but—just a minute, Natalie. What?" I heard him call out. "I've got to get off the phone," he said, then, "How did you manage to get your own line?"

"Just strength of character in action," I said.

He laughed. "Maybe I'll see you in the morning."

"You might. If you're lucky. Bye, bye."

We hung up. Oh, great. I had done it again . . . come off sounding flippant, as though Noel was just another of my friends. But then, that's all he was. And probably all he ever would be. Because of Michelle. He even worried about whether she was happy or not.

I wandered into my bathroom to get a glass of water.

"Look at you," I said to myself in the mirror. "Do you look pale and wan and full of woe?" Not exactly. I looked perfectly normal. Gorgeous, in fact. (Choo Choo and I were always saying how gorgeous we were.) Nothing about my looks gave any clue about the terrible times I was going through.

But oh, poor Michelle (who was truly gorgeous) had to model and make a lot of money. So of course she suffered just tons, and it showed. Showed enough to worry Noel. Enough to make him call *me*.

But wait—he'd really called about his parents making a big deal about the quints. Hadn't he?

I set down the glass. Or had that been only an excuse to call? Nyah. Noel didn't need an excuse. Friends just called.

I sat on the edge of the tub for a minute to think things through. Noel liked me as a friend. That's all it would ever be. So take it or leave it.

I got up. I'd take it. A new friend who was a boy wasn't all that bad. I went to my desk, slid onto the chair and opened my math book. Whether it was just friendship or not didn't matter anyway. I'd be leaving them all behind, all my friends, one of these days. Actually, it now looked like quite a few days. But eventually I'd go to live with Mother. Say good-bye forever to all this turbulence.

A little worrying thought edged into my mind. What was it? Oh, learning French. What a fool I'd been to try to use learning that language as a bargaining agent. Mother had turned it right around and now I'd have to do it, and on my own! If I didn't, it would just go to prove that I hadn't been sincere. That I'd used it as a bribe, which of course I had.

I turned pages to find the math problems. Too bad I didn't know some French person who'd talk and let me learn without brain burnout. No such luck. Except for my mom, I'd never met a single person who spoke French. That proved something. If speaking a foreign language was so great, how come more people didn't do it?

I attacked the math. It went pretty well, except that I kept seeing Noel's face in the margins. When I finished the problems, I went to my closet and checked out my clothes. I wished I had something new and smashing to wear tomorrow, just in case I met him. Oh well, there was the pale yellow cable-knit sweater I hadn't worn yet this fall. I could combine it with the brown plaid skirt. And I could sweep my hair to the side and anchor it with the butterfly clip.

So much to all that. I took out my lenses and got into the shower.

*   *   *

The next morning I was about to open the front door when Dad said, "Natalie, wait a minute."

I glanced at the clock. Noel should be leaving his house about now. "Yes, Dad." I rolled my eyes upward and sighed. "I'll be home right after school, don't worry. 'Bye."

"Would you just hang on for a minute?" he asked, with not much patience. "There's something I want to ask you."

"What."

"Do you have any plans for Saturday night?"

My birthday. Now, surely he wasn't going to ask me to baby-sit on the night of . . . "Why?" I gave him a steady look.

"You and Jean and I have been invited to Toots and Horace's for dinner. To celebrate a big occasion." He smiled. "And then we thought we'd all take in a movie."

Chills and thrills. "That sounds good," I said.

"Okay. I just wanted to let you know."

Jean came into the hall, shifting her briefcase from one hand to the other as she put on her coat. "Jack, did you call the studio to confirm that appointment?" she asked. And as Dad looked blank, she added, "You said you would. Jack, for the photos! Of the quints!"

"Not yet," Dad said. Obviously he had forgotten.

"Honey, there's not much time. We have to do it Saturday." She looked slightly irritated. "Don't you remember? The photographer said he'd set aside two hours, but we'd have to let him know for sure."

"All right, I'll call," Dad said. "As though I didn't have enough other things to do at work."

"Can I go now?" I asked. I could see an argument building, and I didn't want to hear it or be a part of it.

"Go, go," Dad said. I went.

Noel, of course, was nowhere in sight.

When I reached the school, Choo Choo was sitting on a low wall in front of the building. "Hi, sleaze," she said. "I've been waiting for you."

"My lucky day."

"Isn't it. Tell me, is it true what I heard?"

"What did you hear?"

"I was just talking with Noel. And wow!"

Wow what? Could he have said he liked me? But why would he say that to Choo Choo? "What are you talking about anyway?" I tried to look indifferent. Choo Choo got up and walked with me into the school.

"He said the TV stations are going to cover the quints' birthday. Right at your house. Maybe they'll get a shot of you, too." She gave me a little squeeze. "I'm so excited for you!"

I pulled away. "Oh, leave me alone."

"What?"

I left Choo Choo standing there, looking puzzled. I shoved through the crowd, walked to my locker, twirled the combination and slammed the door open. I was sick of it, sick, sick, sick. Now all my friends, even Noel, were caught up in quint fever. Well, I wasn't. I could hardly wait until the time came when I could be rid of the little darlings for good.

I went through the day feeling worse by the minute. There was no one I could talk to now. No one. Not even Noel. I had thought he might be just a little bit

95

interested in me as a person, but no, he was like everyone else. I guess that's what hurt the worst.

At lunch hour, I was a little late. Michelle and Jiggs and Choo Choo were already at the table, with my spot reserved as usual. They were leaning forward, yakking away, but as soon as I came up they pulled back, and got the kind of innocent looks that showed they'd been talking about me.

"We've been discussing the birthday," Michelle said, hesitantly. And then, from the way she gave a little jerk and looked startled, I knew Choo Choo had kicked her under the table.

"Yeh, discussing Michelle's birthday party and that wimp Trish," Jiggs said, lying through her teeth. She went on, "I don't know who was more disgusting, Trish or Troy."

"Oh, Trish, definitely," Choo Choo said. "I hear she's going to try out for the play. Isn't that a riot? She couldn't act her way out of a paper bag."

"Sure she could," Jiggs said. "She acts all the time. She acts like a real scuzz."

"What play are you talking about?" Michelle wanted to know.

"My dear, haven't you heard?" Choo Choo almost gasped. "Eighth grade is doing *Time Out for Ginger*. I thought *everyone* knew! Tryouts are next week, and I think we should all read for a part. It'll be such a lark!"

"Forget it." Jiggs slurped the last drop of milk from her carton. "Basketball tryouts are next week."

"Oh, you're so physical." Choo Choo turned her gaze to me. "How about you, Natalie?"

"It depends." I was finding it hard to swallow. I

could also see that I was making them all uneasy. With a mumbled, "Sorry, I've got to leave," I picked up my tray, turned and got up, and slammed right into Ms. Bredlow.

"Oh, sorry!" Nothing spilled. My eyes almost did though, with tears. I didn't know why. Everything just seemed so out of kilter.

Ms. Bredlow walked with me to the table where we put our trays. Then she touched her hand to my shoulder. "Natalie, you know you're on the schedule to have a conference with me. I was just going to post the list. When could you come in?"

"Anytime." I didn't care.

She glanced at her watch. "Do you have a free hour this afternoon?"

"I have a study hall. Sixth period."

"Good. Get a pass, will you? And I'll see you then."

I was never crazy about these meetings with the counselor. In fact, I usually dreaded them because I had nothing much to say. Today, though, the words poured out like crazy.

Ms. Bredlow listened. It was her job, of course, but for the first time in any of my conferences, she seemed today like an older friend. A friend who cared.

I told her about my life at home, how my father was constantly criticizing me and making demands, and how Jean, even though she was understanding, had little time for me these days.

"Have you tried talking to them, explaining how you feel?" Ms. Bredlow asked.

"It wouldn't do any good. Even if they saw my side

of it, what could they do? The quints need a lot of attention. And get it.''

Her eyes full of concern, Ms. Bredlow asked, ''Do you blame the quints?''

''Not really. They're just babies. It's not *their* fault they were born. Anyway, they're here, and there's nothing anyone can do about it.''

''Have you talked with your mother?''

''Yes.''

''And what does she say?''

''I told her I wanted to go live with her after all, but she said she's too busy with school and classes and things right now.''

''Does leaving seem to be the only answer to you?''

''I don't know. What do you think?''

''Natalie, I can't advise you. All I can do is help you sort things out. But it's your decision.''

''Yeh.'' Oh, great. I might as well talk to a tree.

Ms. Bredlow picked up a pen and clicked the point in and out. ''Let me ask you something, Natalie. It's not your situation, but still . . .'' She put down the pen and faced me again. ''Suppose an older girl, for one reason or another, has a disagreeable home life. She knows a man who says, 'Marry me and I'll take you away from this mess.' What do you think she should do?''

''Is the guy good-looking?''

She laughed. ''Natalie, that's not the issue.'' She waited.

''I don't know.''

''Then let me put it this way. Should a girl run *away* from something or run *to* something?'' She gazed at me. ''There's a difference.''

98

"Yeh, I guess."

"So think about it, Natalie. Okay?" She gave me her most winning smile.

"Yes, I'll think about it. Thanks."

I left. Super. I might have known the counselor would be no help at all. A girl running off to get married had nothing to do with my problems. Ms. Bredlow just had marriage on her mind. She was probably hoping Coach Collins would take *her* away from all this . . . the grubby school and the rotten teenagers with their troubles.

I put our conversation out of my mind during the rest of the day and while getting through dinner, and even during homework time. But as I lay in bed later that night, just as I was in that half-dreamy state before sleep, a thought drifted through my mind. Did I want to run into my mother's arms because I didn't want to be with Dad anymore? Or was it because I wanted to be with her? The thought hovered for a moment and then disappeared.

What did it matter *why?* I just wanted to go as soon as Mother would have me. That was all.

13

——————□■◇■□——————

Mrs. Winkleman tried to do her best with the quints, but as far as I could tell, she kept them in their room all day, like prisoners. When I came home, they'd crowd around the gate. Some of them shook it almost off its hinges, while the rest held out their arms to me in a pleading way and whined, "Lee . . . Lee . . ."

"Let's let them out for a while," I'd say to the sitter. She didn't mind, as long as I was around to help her chase or entertain them. But as soon as I went upstairs, back they'd go in the cage.

Sometimes I'd take the babies, two at a time, up to my room. I'd bounce them on the bed, or crawl around on the floor, pretending to be a dog, chasing them. They'd crawl off in their funny little fanny-waggling way, looking back and chuckling. It was sad to think that such a dopey game was the highlight of their day.

When I'd haul the pair downstairs again and take another two, the deserted ones would scream for a while and poor Mrs. Winkleman would have to distract them. I wondered if the quints might be better off if I ignored them totally, but somehow that seemed so heartless. Ms. Bredlow had asked if I blamed the quints for my problems. No, of course not. It wasn't their fault they'd been born in a batch and were hard to handle because of that.

I always took Emma upstairs last, by herself, and kept her the longest. She'd been the littlest of the quints when they were born and still seemed daintier than the others. And the sweetest, too. When I held her, she'd often pat my cheek and sometimes press her lips against it. None of the quints knew exactly how to kiss, but Emma came the closest.

Thursday night, Jean managed to come home early and prepare a normal, B.Q. dinner. "Wow, Jeanie, you are one great cook," Dad said, scarfing up the veal scallopini. "What's the occasion?"

"Honey!" Jean looked slightly distressed. "Did you forget that this is the night we go shopping? For birthday outfits?"

Dad put down his fork. "That's tonight? My pilot show comes on at eight-thirty. Can we make it back by then?"

I felt sorry for Jean. She looked frustrated as she glanced at the clock. It was already a quarter to seven. "I'll go," I said.

"You would?" Jean's face lighted up. "That's wonderful, Natalie. That would be super." And now, happily, "Anyway, you have better taste and would be more help than someone I could mention."

"You're absolutely right," Dad agreed, digging into the food again.

* * *

101

The choice of clothes for one-year-olds was staggering. We walked up and down the aisle, finding each new bunch cuter than the one before. Jean's face glowed, and I realized what a treat this was for her. She never got to buy a whole batch of clothes for the kids.

We finally picked out four favorites and then got it down to two. Talk about indecision! The red outfits with their white ruffled collars were adorable, but then so were the pale blue ones with animal appliqués across the front. Jean kept looking from one to another. She couldn't seem to make a choice. Finally I had a bright idea.

"Why don't you hold off on the red ones until the Christmas holidays? Then you could drop a hint to your mother or Toots that the quints need new outfits more than new toys."

"Natalie, you're a child genius! That's exactly what I'll do." She put back the red dress and suit and we pulled out two blue boys' outfits and three blue girls' and took them to the sales desk.

The clerk was an older woman with glasses hanging from a chain around her neck. She swung them into position, picked up the clothes and checked the tags. Then she looked at us, puzzled. I knew she was wondering why we were buying five outfits, all in the same size, but neither Jean nor I made any comment. We'd learned not to reveal we had quintuplets because people got all excited and started asking lots of questions like, "How do you manage?" and "What's it like?" Stuff like that. Once, someone even asked for Jean's autograph!

When we left with the package, Jean said, "No

matter what your dad says, I'm going to get at least one new set of toys for the babies. I mean, what's a birthday without presents?''

"Right," I said, thinking of my own birthday. No one had asked me what I wanted. Had they forgotten it was gift time for big sister, too? Probably.

It wasn't such a job to select toys. There were only a few that the quints didn't already have. People loved buying them playthings. Jean checked the jack-in-the-boxes for sharp corners or paint that might flake. They were okay. I insisted on buying some floppy frogs, even though Jean said I should save my money. When we took the items to the counter, the clerk, a bored-looking man this time, wrote up the order, looking even more bored, but not one bit curious.

Since the stores didn't close for an hour, and neither Jean nor I was in all that great a hurry to get home, we strolled around for a while. Jean found a striped scarf to go with her navy suit, and then checked through the woman executive section without buying anything.

From there we went to the teen department, which had platforms and neon tubing and really great rock music blasting from every direction. When I held up a pink wool skirt and oversized matching top and studied the effect in the mirror, I was hoping Jean would say, "That's really you. Let's buy it for your birthday." But instead, she looked at her watch and said, "Natalie, we'd better get going."

Although I'd made it a point to leave the house the last couple of days at the time when Noel should be walking by, I hadn't seen him. Had he figured out the time, too, and left early to avoid me? Why would he do that? What had I done?

And then, when I got to school Friday, I knew why he'd never been in sight. He was standing just inside the entrance, talking to Michelle. They'd probably arranged to reach school early so they could spend a few precious minutes together. Wonderful.

My intention was to slip by fast, before they noticed, but I wasn't fast enough. They saw me and came over, but instead of walking along with me to the lockers, they stopped. So I had to stop too, to avoid seeming rude.

"Hi guys, what's up?" I asked.

"We were just . . . uh . . ." Michelle looked to Noel for help.

"Talking about the play," Noel said. "Choo Choo says she's going to try out."

Was this supposed to be a great news break? "She told us she was," I said, "about a week ago." I turned and looked at Michelle. "You were there."

Michelle was an absolute zero when it came to faking. All she did now was flutter her long, thick eyelashes, perhaps to cool her flushed cheeks, and again look to Noel for help.

"What part will she be trying out for, do you know?" Noel asked. I didn't get it. Why were they asking these dumb questions?

"I haven't the least idea, since I don't know the play," I said, and started off. Noel got in front of me and walked backward, talking a lot of gibberish. When we were about to round the corner, he gave a look down the corridor and stopped, smiling a big smile. Had he gone crazy or what?

And then I saw. Several yards down, a bunch of balloons I could simply not believe were fluttering from strings attached to my locker. I had never seen so many for anyone's birthday—and these balloons were special. Instead of hanging loose, like the ordinary kind, they were filled with helium and strained upward like a big, fat bouquet.

I just stood there, shaking my head and saying, "Wow." Kids came from all directions, crowding around me and shouting "Happy Birthday!"

Then Choo Choo, in her actressy way, came forward and draped a streamer around me, Miss America style, only this one said, *World's Greatest Birthday*.

"Natalie, you must wear this all day," she said. "Except of course, in the shower after gym."

Naturally I took off the banner before entering the first class, but it gave me a glow to think my friends, at least, remembered my birthday, even if it was a day early.

The girls salvaged the few balloons that had survived the roving mobs of the morning and fastened them to my chair at lunch.

"You guys . . . thanks again. I was really surprised," I said.

"We wanted to have a party," Jiggs said, mooshing the catsup around on her hamburger. "But your . . . uh . . . Jean said you had plans."

"Plans?" Then I remembered. Whoop-de-do. Dinner at Toots and Horace's. "Oh, well, you know how families are. But frankly, I'd rather have gone the party route." Smiling, I said, "Especially if Trish and Troy were there. What a fun party pair they'd make!"

I meant it as a joke of course, but too late I noticed

105

the hurt look on Michelle's face. Great. She must have thought I was making fun of her party. But lately it didn't seem to matter what you said; Michelle always got that wounded expression. I could see why Noel wondered about her.

For my birthday breakfast the next day, Jean made pink pancakes. It wasn't a big deal, just red food coloring in the batter, but it gave the Saturday a rosy start. Even the quints got to have pancakes, cut into pieces they could pick up, but without butter or syrup. They didn't know the difference.

"Honey, the day you were born was the happiest day of my life," Dad said. "I'll never forget it."

"I thought your wedding day was the happiest," I said. That's what he'd told Mother a long time ago. As soon as I said it, I felt like scooting under the table, but Jean only smiled. I guess she thought I meant *her* wedding day.

"Well!" Dad drained his coffee cup and clanged it down on the saucer. "We'd better get moving if we're going to be at the photographer's by ten. Can you go along, Natalie, and help keep things reasonably calm?"

"Okay," said the good-natured birthday girl. "Are we dressing up the quints here or what?"

"We'd better wait until we get there," Jean said. "You know what can happen in just seconds." We did.

By the time the quints were all pottied and dressed in their terry-cloth jumpsuits, we didn't have much time to spare. Jean put the new outfits, freshly ironed, in one big box. We gathered up the quints, shoved them into their sweaters, and got into the car.

The photographer had his wife there to help, and it was a good thing. The plan was to photograph each child individually, and then do a group shot. While the guy was getting camera and lights ready, his wife positioned a single quint on a little bench covered with a blue cloth. Naturally, that quint wanted to be with the others, and the others wanted to be on the bench. When the photographer was ready, and the quint settled down, the photographer's wife squeaked toys and made funny sounds, trying to coax cute expressions.

To keep things straight, the quints were being photographed in alphabetical order, which made Alice number one. At first, the four left waiting were fascinated by the sights and sounds of this new place, but by the time we got to Emma, the 'leftovers' were restless and whining because we kept them from running around.

When all five had finally been photographed, the adults were exhausted. But if the single shots had been a battle, taking all of the quints together was a full-scale war. They just wouldn't stay put. The photographer had clustered them on a platform, but Drew jumped off and Beth followed suit. Emma fell off and whimpered, then Craig pushed Alice off and she howled.

The photographer looked at Dad. "How do you handle this, day after day?"

"It's not easy," Dad said, scooping up Alice and quieting her howls.

"I'm trying to think of a way to keep them in a

bunch," the man said, and when I suggested a rope, he answered, "It would show in the picture."

The woman finally came up with five different squeak toys and while the quints sat, examining these new items, her husband got a few shots. Then, battle-weary, but game, he asked if we'd like a family portrait.

"You must be kidding," Dad said.

"Oh, let's," Jean said. "Goodness knows when we'll have another chance. Come on, Natalie."

I wished I'd fixed up myself a little more, but I put on fresh lipstick and fluffed out my hair and let it go at that.

Jean and Dad sat at the ends, with me in the middle. Each of us held one of the girls—I got Emma—and the boys stood in front. To everyone's surprise, these shots went very smoothly. They turned out well, too. Everyone was smiling, as though this was just another happy day in the quint household.

That afternoon, when the mail came, there were birthday cards for me from various relatives, and a big one from Mother. *I miss my darling daughter very much on her special day*, she wrote. *Next year I hope we'll be together*.

Next year!

But for now, I send my love. Oh, yes, and a gift. It should be there by now. Kisses, Mother.

The gift wasn't there. And so far, there were no presents from Jean or Dad, either.

It was fun at Toots and Horace's after all. For one thing, the quints were home with a sitter. For another, the food was definitely for adults with all their teeth.

Just as Toots brought out the triple-layer devil's food cake with swirly white icing and the candles all lighted, the phone rang.

"Ignore it," Toots said. "It's just one of my square-dance women, calling about the contest next week."

After everyone sang "Happy Birthday," I made a wish (Noel, are you receiving?) and blew out the candles. The phone rang again.

"Oh, botheration," Toots said. "I wish that addle-brained Sophie would call someone else for a change." She rose from her chair. "I'll get rid of her fast. Start cutting the cake, Natalie."

I had just flopped the first piece onto the plate when Toots returned. "It's for you, Jean. The sitter."

With a distressed look, Jean got up and went to the kitchen.

"What was it?" Dad asked, when she returned.

"Oh, nothing." Jean tried to smile. "Mmmmm, that cake looks good."

After we'd eaten, Horace left the table and came back with three packages, one small, one big, and one enormous. "I wonder who these could be for," he said. "Well, well, Natalie, I guess it's you."

I dived at the small one first. It was a pair of earrings . . . for pierced ears! "Great!" I said. "Oh, thanks, Jean."

"I can exchange them if . . . if you don't want to get your ears pierced," she said.

"No way!" Mom hadn't been in favor of it, but that was nearly two years ago.

The next box, the big one, was from Toots and Horace. I gasped when I saw the pink wool skirt and top. "But how did you know?" And then I looked at Jean and saw her smile. "You told them!"

I held the top to me and everyone said it was just my color. "I guess I know how to shop," Toots said. "Eh, kid?"

Dad said, "What about the last one?" I leaped at the huge package, stripped away the wrappings, and then stared, wordless. It was a suitcase! I couldn't help wondering if Dad was trying to tell me something, like *leave*.

"Remember last summer," he said, breaking the silence, "when you went to your mother's and had to use my suitcase because you said yours was too babyish? And small?"

"Yeh. This is just the kind I wanted, Dad." I unzipped it. "It sure is roomy. I can get all my clothes in it and have room left over for—"

He finished the sentence for me. "Hair dryer, hot comb, all that junk you put on your face . . ."

"It's big enough to hold a bird cage," Toots said. "And I just love the maroon color."

"I do, too," I said, trying to sound really pleased. "Thanks a lot, Dad."

"Now," Toots said, getting up. "How about some coffee to go with another slice of cake?"

"Oh, I don't think we should," Jean said in a hesitant way. "Jack, the sitter . . ."

"What about her?"

"Well, she thinks Alice has a fever. And she threw up her supper."

"Oh, no!" Dad said. "Wouldn't you know. Our one night out."

"I'm sorry," Jean said to Toots and Horace. "It

was all so nice up to now. But why don't you all go on with the party, and then to the movie? I'll run home and see what's what.''

"We'd better both leave," Dad said. "If one's sick, the others will follow. What a life."

I was going to go with them, but Toots and Horace insisted on taking me to the movie.

I couldn't help thinking that this wasn't the greatest birthday of the ages, but yet it hadn't been all that bad. First, the balloons and the big fuss made over me by my friends, then the presents and the dinner and cake at Toots and Horace's. Next year, if I were with Mom, it could be a whole lot quieter.

Toots came out, wearing her square-dance wig for the occasion. "What movie are we going to see?" I asked her.

"Makes no difference to me, as long as it's not one of those kid shows," she said. "Let's pick one with some love and action."

"All *right!*" I said. It looked to me as though this birthday might end on a high note after all.

14

—————— ○■○■○ ——————

Sunday was a terrible day, with three quints sick and the two others acting like little beasts. Then suddenly, on Sunday night, the fevers dropped, the barfing stopped, and even the animal behavior tapered off. It was at least ten o'clock, though, before we got all the quints quieted and in bed. By that time Jean and Dad and I were hanging on the ropes.

On Monday, when I got home from school the gift from Mother had arrived. It was heavy. Could it be, could it be? It was! Oh Mom! She truly loved me, she had to, to get me something she herself didn't care for one bit. It was a silver stereo/recorder, with all kinds of levers and two speakers and a tape deck. I plugged it in, checked out the instructions, and had it blasting away in no time. What a sound!

I stretched out on my bed and wallowed in the depth of tone coming from the speakers. After I'd played two cassettes I got up to root around for some more. My glance happened to fall on the French tapes, which I'd taken out of the box but never actually played.

Maybe, with this new stereo, they'd get me interested, though that seemed unlikely. I slipped one into the slot and tried to concentrate on it. Happily, the phone rang halfway through the first lesson. I turned down the sound and answered. It was Noel!

"What are you doing?" he asked. "I mean, I hope I'm not interrupting something vital—like math." He laughed.

I hesitated, and then thought, why not? "Actually, I was listening to my French tapes." That sounded terribly intellectual and should impress Noel.

"French? I didn't know you knew the language."

I hesitated again and then admitted, "I don't, actually. That's why I have these tapes. It's a study course."

"Well, I'm impressed." So I'd been right!

"To tell the truth, I'm only doing it to please my mother," I said. "She teaches French, and has been after me for years to learn."

"Why didn't you learn it from her?"

"Too stubborn. I wish now that I had."

"It *is* a lot easier to pick it up casually. I didn't even have to try."

"Noel, are you saying *you* speak French?"

"Of course."

"But how come?" This was unbelievable!

He laughed. "I'm from Canada, remember, where there are lots of French-Canadians. My mother, for one."

"And you just picked it up?"

"Sure. Half the time my mother speaks French, around the house."

"Wow. I wonder if . . . no, I guess not."

"You wonder *what?*"

"I was going to say I wondered if I could, like, hang around her and pick it up, too, but that's crazy. Forget I said it."

"You could hang around *me.*"

I felt a pulse in my throat for an instant. "Sure," I said, "that would do it." And then to let him know I knew he was kidding, I said, "How come you called, huh? Having problems with math, science, home ec?"

"Yes, especially home ec." He cleared his throat. "I really called to get the lowdown on basketball tryouts. They're tomorrow for you, too, aren't they?"

"Yep. What did you want to know?"

"How tough they are and how long they go on."

"Oh. Well, lots of kids try out, so they hold them two nights, after school. You aren't worried, are you?"

"Not really. To tell the truth, I'd rather not even get on the team. My dad, though, was a big athlete and kind of expects me to follow the same path."

So Noel got leaned on at home, too. I'd never have guessed it. "What would your father do if you told him you didn't want to make the team?"

"He'd ask me what I'd rather do, and then not believe me when I told him."

"What would you rather do?"

"You won't believe it, either." He paused. "I'd like to try out for the play."

I couldn't believe it. "But why? Why would you want to do a—"

"Silly thing like that? I don't know. I've never done any acting, but it sounds like fun. And after all I was named for Noel Coward. You know who he was, don't you? A playwright and an actor. So it's really my parents' fault, or at least my mother's. She's the one who chose the name.''

"Hmmm." What could I say to all this?

"I'm not sure I'd be any good, though. I'm not even sure I could memorize the lines."

"Memorizing lines is easy. It must be, if Choo Choo can do it. I helped coach her one other time she was in a play."

"Would you coach me? Hey, how about a trade-off? You help me with lines, I'll help you with French."

"Okay." Wow, I thought. What a good excuse to spend time with Noel!

"First, though, I've got to get cast. No, before that I've got to run the idea past my dad and get his reaction." Noel paused and then went on, "I don't know why I'm making a big deal of it. My father's cool . . . likes us to try new things. I guess your dad's the same way."

"Oh, sure, he always backs me up," I lied.

"So the real reason I called . . ."

I waited.

He laughed. "I just wanted to talk. Okay?"

"Sure." I laughed a little, too.

"So. Well, now that we've talked . . ."

". . . Now that we've talked . . ."

"Good niiiiight . . . Natalie."

"Good niiiiight . . . Noel."

We laughed once again and hung up.

I flicked on the French tapes and flopped back on the floor. The foreign phrases flowed out of the speakers and right past my mind. The only words I could think of were the ones Noel had just spoken to me.

I had hated it when Dad was a pilot and sometimes had to sleep during the day, and got irritable when there was too much noise. But now it was worse. He was always around in the morning, and that's when most of our fights happened.

Like on Tuesday. All I said was that I'd be home late because of basketball tryouts, and Dad threw a fit.

"Is there ever any stretch of time when you're not involved in something?" he asked. "Can't you be content for a little while without being some kind of sports star?"

"I'm not exactly a star," I said angrily. "How can I be, when I have to cut practice all the time?"

"There wasn't much soccer cutting that I could see. You were always turning up late."

I looked at Jean, expecting her to come to my defense as usual, but instead, she said, "Natalie, I know tryouts are important. But I'm wondering, I don't know, if you could skip them this once?"

"Why?" This wasn't fair. "Don't you think Mrs. Winkleman can handle the quints by now?"

"Sure, on an ordinary day," Jean said, emptying the coffeepot. "But tonight's going to be like gangbusters, with the newspaper and TV people all over the place. I was hoping you could help keep the quints calmed down." She sighed. "Wow, I'm not looking forward to it."

"Well, Jeanie, you're the one who was all for press coverage," Dad said, taking his dishes to the sink.

If I'd wanted to get Dad really steamed, I'd have reminded him that he was the one who'd talked to the press. "What time will they be here?" I asked, grudgingly.

"Around four," Jean said. "I'm taking off at noon, to see that the house looks halfway decent, and to get the quints dressed. I sure wish Toots was in town."

I wished it, too. But no one had asked *her* to give up square dancing. "All right, I'll come home. But just remember, I won't be here tomorrow night."

"Thanks, honey," Jean said. "What would we do without you?"

When I rounded the corner after school and our house came in sight, I have to admit I felt a surge of excitement. There was a TV-unit truck in our driveway, plus three cars. Neighbors were standing in bunches on the sidewalk, staring at our front windows.

"What's going on, Natalie?" Mrs. Spenser called out. "Why is the TV here?"

"To cover the quints' birthday. Big deal." I grinned.

"That's so exciting!" Jane Taylor exclaimed. "Aren't you thrilled?"

"I guess." I gave them a little wave and went inside. Wow! The lights almost blinded me. I stumbled over a big snakelike cable on the floor.

"Watch it, sis," some guy with a camera said. "Stay back."

If Jean had straightened up the house, it was wasted effort. Nothing was where it should have been. The babies' cribs had been dismantled and were stacked in the hall. The clothes from the "bookcases" were now on the stairway. Even the easy chairs and lamp had

117

been moved from the room. The extension gate had been taken from its hinges, but there was no danger of the quints getting out. The doorway was full of equipment and there were at least eight people milling around.

I could hear one quint crying . . . it sounded like Beth. I strained to see into the room and saw the babies all in a bunch, with Jean trying to calm them. Just then she spotted me.

"Oh, Natalie," she called, with relief showing on her face. "Could you come in and help me settle them down?"

A photographer moved to let me through.

"This is their big sister," Jean explained to the crew. "She is just marvelous with the quints."

"Sometimes I am." I went over and knelt down. "What's the matter, Beth?"

Magically, the little girl stopped crying and threw her arms around me. "It's all right, Natalie's here," I said into her hair.

"Nancy, could you get them to look toward the camera?" one of the TV guys asked. "Or better yet, get them doing something?"

What was I, a puppeteer? I looked around for their toys and spotted the jack-in-the-boxes. Between us, Jean and I got the quints interested in the toys and then edged out of camera range. "Where's Dad?" I whispered.

"Out in the kitchen, giving an interview. Oh, Craig!"

"Don't stop him, Ma'am. Good action."

Wonderful. Craig was simply bopping his brother on the head with poor Jack.

118

As the quints got tired of the toys and started toddling around, the guy with the hand-held camera squatted down and followed.

"I'd like to get some close-ups," another cameraman said, "but even with the zoom, it does no good if they turn their backs. I wonder if the mother could pick each one up?"

So Jean lifted each quint in turn while I called out and got them to look toward the camera. "Nice going, Nancy," the guy said.

"It's Natalie." He paid no attention. I mean, who was *I*?

A pretty red-haired woman who was standing next to me said, "What do you call the quints, Natalie?"

"Pests."

She laughed. "I mean, do you have any pet names for them? Or nicknames?"

"No, we gave them short names purposely, so they couldn't be changed into anything else." And then I continued, "When they were first born their cribs in the hospital were labeled A, B, C, D and E. So we used those letters for their names."

"Clever." The woman chattered away for a while and then they all started packing up their equipment to leave. The newspaper people hung around, though, taking an unbelievable number of pictures.

Dad, who'd joined us, finally said, "Isn't that about enough? You've surely got some decent shots by now."

"Just a few more." A guy with a self-powered camera kept clicking away. "These kids are dynamite."

Jean went forward. "Please. It'll take hours to settle

119

them down, after all this.'' She had to laugh, though, as Drew put a floppy frog on his head and looked up at it cross-eyed. "Come on, they're getting crazy.'' She went to the quints, and the photographer, smiling, put away his camera. "You ought to sign them up with some modeling agency,'' he said. "You'd make a fortune . . . really clean up.''

"Never,'' Jean said firmly.

A lucky break for the quints, I thought. *To have been born to Jean, and not to Michelle's mother. There's a woman who would really have cleaned up if they were hers.*

15

―○■○○―

"Oh man," Jiggs said to me the next day, "you blew it. I never saw so many people at tryouts. Really tough competition. You should never have skipped."

"I'll be there today."

"Good luck," Jiggs said. "You'll need it."

"I can see you have gobs of faith in me."

"All I'm saying is you missed out on the first round, and you know how Coach Collins feels about dedication and stuff like that."

When I showed up after school I saw what Jiggs meant by competition. It looked as though every girl in the three gym classes was there for tryouts, all except Choo Choo and Michelle. While waiting to get started we took practice shots and dribbled the ball down the court. Trish came bouncing by and threw me one of her phony smiles.

When Coach Collins appeared, he blew his whistle and told us to line up in two rows, facing each other. We did, and passed the ball back and forth as fast as we could.

After that, we formed other groups and raced up and shot baskets. Collins had us going for about an hour. It was strenuous and we all made mistakes. I hoped he was looking somewhere else when I made mine.

When the coach finally blew his whistle to signal the end of the tryout, we sprawled on the floor, sweaty, exhausted, but with hope in our pounding hearts.

"I saw some good work out there today," Collins said. "There's enough material for at least three teams, but we have to cut it down to two. As you know, the first team will play major games, and the second team will play—"

"—in second rate games," Jiggs muttered to me.

"—their scheduled games and will also stand by to substitute in case of injury to any member of the first team. I will now read off the names of the second team."

Jiggs whispered, "Doesn't this remind you of the Miss America contest? The third runner-up, the second . . ."

"Ssshhh." I elbowed her. "He's reading the names."

When he finished, and our names weren't on it, Jiggs gave me a light punch on the arm. "We've gone and made the first team again."

"Trish's name wasn't called, either."

"We'll take care of her. Just a little injury."

Jiggs' name was the second one called for the first team.

"Hold the applause," she whispered, "until all names are announced."

The coach read the third name, the fourth, and

suddenly he had read them all. And my name wasn't one of them!

I sat there in shock. Jiggs didn't say anything for a minute, either. Then she said, "There must be some mistake."

I had a strange taste in my mouth. Of course I knew the expression, *the sweet smell of success*. Well, now I knew the awful taste of defeat.

"At least," Jiggs said in an unusually subdued voice, "Trish didn't make it either."

It didn't help. Who cared about Trish? I hadn't made the team. I hadn't even made the second team! Now I understood how the rejects of beauty pageants felt when the curtain closed to hide their disappointed looks. Only here, there was no curtain.

The winners, now on their feet, were screeching and hugging each other. The losers were slinking off to the showers.

"Hey," Jiggs said as we started to leave the gym, "I'll drop out. Who needs to play this lousy game anyway?"

"You will not drop out. I'd hate it if you did something weird like that and besides . . ." I stopped. Collins was walking up to us.

"Sorry, Wentworth," he said. "You're a good player, one of the best."

"Then why didn't you take her?" Jiggs demanded. I'd have kicked her under the table, only there wasn't any table.

Ignoring Jiggs, the coach said, "I can't count on you. You've skipped practices, important practices, and you didn't even show up for first night tryouts. To me, that shows a lack of dedication."

"I have . . . problems at home," I mumbled.

"That's too bad. So work on your problems and get them squared away before next year. That's all I can say."

He walked on, and under her breath, Jiggs said, "Meathead, we won't be here next year. We're eighth-graders, remember?"

"Let it go, Jiggs," I said, walking toward the showers. "It doesn't matter. I'll find something else to do instead."

"Yeh, like what?"

I shrugged but didn't answer. What I was thinking was, *I'll go home like a dutiful little daughter and quint-sit. What else?* And wouldn't that please my father! Why should he care about my humiliation? Would it bother him when kids around school asked why I wasn't on the team? Not at all.

And then I got another thought. How could I tell Noel that I was a loser because of my dad, when on the phone I'd said he always backed me up?

It wasn't fair! It just wasn't fair the way my dad was running my life . . . and ruining it!

When I got home, I let myself into the house very quietly and made no sound as I unlatched the gate to go upstairs. When I got to my room, the phone was ringing.

"Yeh?" I kicked off my shoes and unzipped my skirt and let it fall to the floor.

"Natalie! I can't believe it!" Choo Choo shrieked. "I'm so thrilled to know you!"

"You don't have to rub it in." Boy, bad news really traveled fast.

"But on TV! I just can't believe it!"

Neither could I. Why would they flash the news about some dumb junior high tryouts? "Get off it, Claudia," I said. "I'm in no mood for your sick humor."

"You Twinkie! Don't you hear what I'm saying? You were on TV! On the five o'clock news—you and the quints!"

I dropped to the bed. "You're kidding."

"I'm not kidding. I saw you myself. You looked absolutely fab!"

"I . . . I don't get it. They didn't do me . . ."

"They certainly did, darling. Some woman asked what you called the quints, and you said, 'Pests.' With a really cute expression on your face. I'm so jealous. You mean you didn't see it?"

"I was at the tryouts. And didn't make the team."

"I'll bet anything they rerun it at ten o'clock. I'm taping it if they do. You ought to, too. They got some cute shots of the quints, bopping around, but you were the absolute highlight!"

In the background I could hear Choo Choo's mother saying something and then Choo Choo said to me, "Hold on, Nat. My mom's just brought in the paper and there's a whole bunch of pictures of the quints and a big headline that says, let's see . . . WENTWORTH QUINTS ONE YEAR OLD. Isn't it exciting to see your name in big headline print?"

"Uh, you're the one looking at it. I don't have the paper."

"Well, get a copy! In fact, rush out and buy several. I'm taking mine to school tomorrow so you can autograph it. Or should I come over now?"

In a way, I wanted to be alone, but in another way, I wanted company. "Come over now. Oh, and Choo Choo, do me a favor and don't make a fuss at school tomorrow. You know how the kids are."

"Oh, do I ever. Be right there!"

Before she arrived, Jiggs called. She'd seen the paper. So had Shannon and Kristen and quite a few others. They all called.

"Did anyone say anything about you being on TV?" Choo Choo asked, coming into my room.

"No, most kids don't watch the news."

"Then why don't you call everyone back and alert them, so they'll watch at ten?" Choo Choo widened her eyes. "If it were me, I'd tell the whole world. Even Trish. Especially Trish." She flopped backward on my bed. "Oh, wow, I'd really love to see her when you flash on that screen, lookin' so good. She's going to grind her teeth down to nubs."

Dad came home with no less than twelve copies of the paper. I've never seen him look so elated. Both he and Jean had caught the telecast at work. "Did you see it, Sparkles?" Dad asked me.

"No, I wasn't home."

"I saw it," Choo Choo spoke up. "The quints were just adorable, Mr. Wentworth. And Natalie here— what a star!"

"That's my girl," Dad said.

Jean, who had just come home, said, "And Natalie, that was a nice picture of you in the paper, too. Even if it was a little blurred."

"What picture?" I leaned to look while Choo Choo began to turn the newspaper pages.

"Not that paper. The weekly. It came out today. Someone brought it to work. Here." Jean dug a clipping out of her purse.

Choo Choo grabbed it first.

"It's you, all right!" she said. "Hey, this is from the soccer team picture. They've blown up just your face, Natalie. That's why it's kind of blurred."

It was a strange feeling to see a picture of *me* in the paper, and pretty wild to read the headline, which said, SISTER OF THE QUINTS. And then a smaller headline, *Not Always Fun and Games, Says Natalie*.

I couldn't believe it. The article described how I tried to lead a normal life, going out for sports at school and keeping up my grades, but life at home had its ups and downs.

"I didn't know you gave an interview," Jean said.

"I didn't! This . . . this reporter made it all up!"

"But it's true," Choo Choo said. "You do try to lead a normal life." Then she gave a little cry. "Natalie! That time you were sick, some woman came and sat by me on the bench. And I remember her asking about you. And I told her some stuff. I forgot all about it until now. So that's how, that's how she got that story. I told her. That makes *me* almost famous!"

"My, my," Dad said. "It seems we're surrounded by celebrities. Hey, speaking of the famous, what's with the quints? I hear no screams, no shouts, no sounds of strife."

"They're zonked out," Jean said. "And it's no wonder, after all that commotion yesterday. I thought we'd never get their room back in order."

"The press people," I explained to Choo Choo,

"really tore up the place, and then they just packed up and left."

"That's the way it always is," Choo Choo said in her most actressy voice.

None of us was really in the mood for an official birthday party for the quints, but as Dad said, we had to do the customary thing.

Actually, it wasn't too bad. Toots and Horace had arrived home during the day and came over not only with a casserole and salad, but also with five small birthday cakes.

It didn't take any coaxing to get Choo Choo to stay, so with the six of us, it made a keeper for each of the quints and one left over to take pictures.

Dad did the regular ones with his self-focus Pentax, and then while the quints totally wrecked the cakes, Horace captured the scene with his movie camera.

By the time it was all finished, the kids had cake and icing on their faces, high chairs, and even in their hair. It was a good thing they didn't have a lot of it—hair, I mean.

Toots did the dishes while Dad and Jean and I dunked the quints and got them into their sleepers. Horace drove Choo Choo home in the meantime, so she'd have time to get her VCR ready for the newscast. "If they don't run those scenes again, I'll shoot myself," she said.

Dad set up our own VCR and we all sat around waiting for the news. We knew right away they were going to do the quints because they announced it as part of the nightly line-up, after a terrorist attack in some place I'd never heard of, and some local gambling raid.

128

I waited, feeling my heart thump, wanting to watch, and yet wanting to cover my eyes. The quints came on, bouncing around and looking more lovable on the screen than in real life, and then . . . oh no . . . came the close-up of me, half-smiling. As the woman's voice said, "What do you call the quints, Natalie?" I smiled more, looked down, then up, and said, "Pests."

Jean squeezed my arm. "Oh, honey, see? You gave it just the touch it needed to keep from being yukky cute."

"Well, I think it *was* cute, all of it," said the proud father of the quints. "Not yukky at all." He was beaming.

"I'm just so proud of all of you," Toots said. "I can hardly wait to lord it over my square-dance folks. This isn't just showing off in some competition. This is the real celebrity thing."

Faintly, I heard my phone ringing. I dashed upstairs and grabbed it. "Hi!"

"Hello, famous one," Noel said. "Are you still speaking to ordinary mortals like myself?"

"As long as you're suitably adoring," I answered. "I guess you caught my act on TV."

"Twice. I tried calling before, but your line was busy. And busy. And busy some more. Then there was a long spell when you just didn't answer."

"My public is so demanding," I said. "Actually, we were partying. Today's the quints' official birthday. I don't want to see, smell or taste icing for the next ten years!"

"I'll bet. Well, it's late. I just wanted to congratulate you before the mob closes in tomorrow. You'd better wear dark glasses to school and speak with a foreign accent.''

"Like French?" It suddenly occurred to me I'd have plenty of time to learn the language, with no basketball after school. I decided I might as well tell Noel and get it over with. "Have you heard?" I asked, casually. "I didn't make the basketball team."

"No?" He answered just as casually. "Then how about trying out for the play with me?"

"I don't think so." I paused. "You're trying out for sure? Your dad doesn't care?"

"Nah, he just kidded around, told my mother that's what she gets for naming me after Noel Coward. You know who really should try out, though?"

"Who?"

"Michelle. It might take away some of her shyness."

I felt a slight twinge of jealousy. "I don't think she ever would. Unless her mother forced her to do it."

"You're probably right. What did Michelle have to say about your big moment on the evening news?"

"She didn't call."

"No? She must not have seen it then. I'm not surprised. Michelle doesn't seem to be with it these days. In any way."

"Are you worried about her?" That just slipped out. *Say no,* I thought.

"Not worried exactly. Just wondering. Listen, star, I've got to hit the books. And I guess you want to keep the lines open in case Hollywood calls."

"Oh, right. I hope all this fame doesn't go to my head."

"It better not. I like my girls humble. Well, so long."

"So long." I hung up and let out a big breath. *His girls!* Was I one of his girls? I must be! And if there were others, they were probably in Canada, so what did I care?

After all that, I couldn't settle down to study. I decided to take a shower instead, and let Noel's words run over me along with the water. As I held my face up to the spray, I thought about his wanting me to try out for the play. I know it had nothing to do with acting ability, he'd simply wanted an excuse to be near me. Hadn't he?

But helping him with lines would be a good excuse. (I was sure he'd land a part.) And he had offered to help me with French. That would be another good excuse for keeping in touch.

As for my not making the team, that would fade away as kids crowded around at school and talked about my being on TV. Even Michelle hadn't done that, except for commercials, and they didn't count.

And my picture in the paper! Wow, wouldn't Trish be jealous. She'd been in that team picture, but they used only my face.

I'd have to remember to send a copy of the paper to Mother. Too bad she couldn't see me on TV. But she could see our copy on the VCR. I turned off the shower and stepped out of the tub. Toweling off, I began thinking that Mother might not really be so thrilled, seeing the quints in action, and my connection with them.

When I lived with her, *if* I lived with her, none of

131

these exciting things would happen. In fact, life with Mom might even be on the dull side.

I got into my pajamas, brushed my hair, and then drifted to my desk to make a few stabs at homework. But it was still hard to settle down. Lately, life had seemed to be just one big event after another. What next, I wondered.

I had no idea that the thing that happened next would shake up the whole family.

16

————◦■◦■◦————

The first call came the next night, at around eight o'clock.

Jean and Dad and I were upstairs. They were watching TV and I was hovering by the door, waiting to see how the show ended before going to my room. When the phone rang, Jean reached over and picked up the receiver.

My glance went from the TV to Jean because of the way she sat bolt upright and then motioned for Dad to turn down the sound. He did. Jean was saying, "Who is this?" in a startled way, and then she took the receiver from her ear, stared at it, puzzled, and then looked at Dad.

"What's the matter?" he asked. "Who was that?"

"I don't know," Jean said in a strange voice.

"Well, what did they say?"

"Just . . . 'You'd better watch out.' "

"What?"

I went over to her. "Is that all they said?"

"Yes. 'You'd better watch out.' What could that mean?"

Dad took the receiver from Jean, listened to the dial tone, and replaced it. "Did you recognize the voice?"

"No. Whoever it was, was disguising it." Her eyes widened. "Oh, Jack!"

"Hey, now." He put an arm around her and pulled her against him. "There's been a lot of publicity about the family. Someone's just trying to be funny. To spook us out. Don't let it get to you, Jeanie."

I half-sat on the arm of the sofa. "That's right, Jean. I've heard about celebrities getting crank calls and letters from people they don't even know. The country's crawling with creeps."

"It sure is," Dad agreed. "Let's forget about it." He kicked up the sound on the TV, but he kept his arm around Jean.

I went back to my room, thinking about the call. It could have been some kid trying to be funny. And then I remembered the way the guys at school had acted that day. Most of them had been wildly impressed by my being on TV, but some were openly envious.

In the locker room before gym class, when several girls crowded around and said they'd seen me, I had noticed Trish and her groupies standing apart. They looked at me, then dipped their heads together and laughed. Afterward, on the gym floor, every one of them made it her business to get near me, hiss "Stuck up" and then take off. What jerks.

"Oh, pity them," Choo Choo had said later, just before we parted in the hall. "The poor dears are beside themselves with envy. Your TV appearance was bad enough, but the icing on the cake was that picture of you in the paper.'' She laughed.

"You were a little teed off yourself," Jiggs reminded her. "Because they used only Natalie's face from that group shot, instead of the whole soccer team's."

"I was not teed off, as you so quaintly put it," Choo Choo said. "I just thought they should have made the effort to get a really good picture of Natalie. I hope they do better by me when I'm a famous actress."

Jiggs made a rude sound.

I changed the subject. "When are the play tryouts?"

"Tomorrow, as a matter of fact. I'm a bundle of nerves."

Choo Choo didn't look a bit nervous. Actually, she was dead sure she'd get a part. I wished I had her confidence.

Now, in my room, I had to hit the books, but that weird phone call had thrown me off a little. I didn't want to talk about it (there wasn't that much to tell) but I did want to talk to someone. Claudia and Jiggs were out, because we'd already yakked for hours after school. I decided to call Noel. I could use wishing him luck in tryouts as an excuse for my phoning.

Thank goodness he answered himself. I didn't want his parents to think I was chasing him.

"Hi," I said. "It's Natalie, star of stage, screen and newspaper. Oh, well, not stage. I don't do live performances."

"You could if you wanted to," he said. His voice was curiously flat.

"I don't want to go into all that again," I said.

"Suit yourself."

Well. He certainly wasn't sounding the way he had

the night before. I wondered if it was something I'd said or done. There was only one way to find out. "Noel . . . is something wrong?" I asked. "If you're upset with me I wish you'd—"

"Why should I be upset with you?" he interrupted. After a brief pause, he said, "Actually, it's about Michelle."

"You're upset with her?"

"No, *about* her. Or concerned, I guess you'd say. Her family stopped by a little while ago, and even my parents noticed how depressed Michelle seems to be. So withdrawn."

"Noel, that girl has never been an extrovert exactly. Like, I mean, the life of the party."

"I'm not talking personality. Just mood. She seems so *down*."

I wasn't feeling so *up* myself. "She'll be okay," I said. "Listen, I've got to do math. Just called to wish you luck in landing a part tomorrow."

"Oh . . . that's right. It's tomorrow."

"Yeh, well 'bye!" I said, and hung up quickly. I felt a flush of annoyance at myself for calling. Noel had probably figured out that I'd just used the tryouts as an excuse. I felt so . . . transparent. And all the while who was Noel thinking about? Why, dear, sweet Michelle who seemed so sad, poor baby. *Noel, you fool, that's the way she is!*

And here, I had thought he liked me because of the way I made him laugh. He hadn't laughed tonight, though, and I felt anything but witty. I felt like a fool, in fact.

Finally, I forced the memory of my stupid call to the back of my mind by doing some heavy-duty studying. By then I had totally forgotten the other call from earlier in the evening. The one that had upset Jean.

The next call came the following night while we were putting the quints to bed. When the phone rang, Dad hoisted Craig in his arms and went to the kitchen to answer. When he came back, his face was flushed with annoyance.

"What is it, Jack?" Jean asked. And then she cried out, "Oh, not another call?"

"If this continues, I'm calling the police." Dad put Craig into his bed.

"What did they say?" Jean looked apprehensive.

"Some gibberish about this being a second warning."

"Oh, Jack! I'm scared!"

I was feeling jittery, myself. "Could you tell what kind of voice it was this time, Dad?"

"It sounded like a woman, but I couldn't be sure."

After they turned everything off except the night light and we left the room, Jean said, "We're getting a burglar alarm." She looked at Dad as though expecting an argument, but he said grimly, "All right, it wouldn't hurt. Not that this is anything except a nut on the loose. But if it'll make you feel better . . ."

The next day I knew Dad had arranged for the alarm because when I got home from school and opened the front door, the blast nearly knocked me over.

Mrs. Winkleman came running, and between her anguished cries of "How did they say to turn this off?" and the quints' shrieks of terror and the alarm still blasting away, the whole neighborhood must have been on the alert. The sitter finally got the thing turned off and between the two of us we managed to quiet the quints.

The calls continued and Dad finally did contact the police and the telephone company. They both said the same thing: "Keep the caller on the line and we'll try to trace it."

"Tell me how we're supposed to keep them on the line," Dad said, "when they just say their piece and hang up?"

Jean began looking pale and drawn.

"Honey," Dad said to her, "you've got to put this out of your mind."

"Out of my mind!" Jean's voice broke. "When someone's threatening our babies?"

"Now, they're not exactly threatening the quints."

"What would you call it then?" she demanded.

"It's just . . . well, how am I supposed to know what it means? I still say it's some nut who gets his jollies out of . . ."

"Or *her* jollies," I said. "Didn't you say it sounded like a woman?"

"I don't care who it is. I just want it stopped." Jean looked ready to burst into tears.

Dad put an arm around her. "Jeannie, getting up and sitting in the quints' room at night, the way you've been doing, isn't going to help. It's just wearing you out. If anyone came prowling around, I'd hear him. Or her. You've got to get your rest."

"Besides," I said, "if anyone even tried to kidnap the quints, those kids would make a racket people would hear in the next county."

138

I realized I shouldn't have said the word *kidnap* because Jean started sobbing. Dad took her in his arms and gave me a dirty look. But wasn't that what it was all about?

If there was anything good about the phone calls, it was the fact that they gave *me* something to talk about during lunch. I was already sick of listening to Jiggs go on about basketball or Choo Choo the play, in which of course she had a leading part. So did Noel.

On Friday, I began talking before anyone else had a chance. "Well, gang," I said, "we got another of those calls last night." Even Michelle, who had made it back to school after missing several days, looked interested.

"My dad's fit to be tied," I said. "And Jean's a wreck."

"No hint of who it is?" Choo Choo asked.

"Nope. I answered last night. It could be anyone."

Suddenly Choo Choo snapped her fingers. "I bet I know!" And while we all stared at her, she said, "Trish."

"Trish?" Jiggs stopped shoving in the food. "Why would she do it?"

Choo Choo looked smug. "My dear, because she's eaten up with jealousy. Over Natalie."

"Natalie?" Jiggs frowned. "Why?"

"Oh, really. Who had her picture in the paper? Who was on TV? Who's the sister of the quints? Ta da!" She held out her palm toward me. "None other than!"

I stared at her. "What does this have to do with the quints? Why would Trish be threatening a bunch of babies?"

"What exactly does the caller say?" Jiggs asked.

139

"Just stuff like, 'You'll be sorry,' or 'This is a warning.' Things like that."

"Oh, she means the quints, all right." Choo Choo was always so sure of being right. She set down her milk. "I've got an idea, Natalie. Tonight when the call comes, you be sure to answer, and say, 'Oh, knock it off, Trish.' See what happens."

Jiggs agreed it was a good idea. I looked at Michelle, but her mind seemed to have drifted off somewhere. I promised Choo Choo and Jiggs that I'd try the Trish tactic.

That same day, after school, Noel caught up with me as I was walking home. I hadn't seen much of him lately.

"No rehearsal today?" I asked, as he fell in step beside me.

"Not on Fridays." He sounded perfectly natural. I guess my phoning the other night hadn't turned him off after all. "What's new in your life?"

I was about to tell him about the threatening calls, when someone came hurrying up to join us. Michelle. Oh, wonderful.

"Michelle . . ." Noel looked more surprised than pleased. "Where are you going?"

"Why, to your house, of course. And then to Natalie's."

We both simply stared at her. Then Noel said, "Any special reason?"

"To see the quints. You know that, Noel."

Before he could protest, she went on, "It's all right. My mother will be there."

140

I couldn't understand what she was babbling about. This was Weird City, with Michelle the mayor.

Noel stopped. "What are you talking about, Michelle?"

She shook her head, as though he was really dense. "Don't you remember? My mother said she'd take your mother to see the quints. You know very well how much she wants to see them."

"You're saying my mother asked your mother?" he said to Michelle. "Why? I mean, why *your* mother?"

"Because she just loves the quints." Michelle made a puzzled frown. "I don't understand that. She doesn't like babies." And then she turned to me. "Did you know Mother threw away Lovey-Baby?"

"Yes, you told me."

We began walking again. Michelle said, "It's a long time since I've seen *your* babies, Natalie. But it will be all right, because my mother will be there."

Noel and I exchanged looks, but didn't say anything as we walked on. I knew he was thinking the same thing I was. Strange, very strange. Our friend Michelle had definitely come a little unwrapped.

17

When we came to our house, Michelle strolled on by. Noel stopped and murmured, "Did you know anything about all this?"

"No. Michelle never even mentioned it at lunch. I wonder why."

"She's off on a cloud somewhere." He shrugged, "Well, I may see you later." He trotted off to catch up with Michelle.

I rang the front doorbell, as I did every day now, to keep from setting off the alarm. After a while, when there was no answer, I went around to the back. Not only were the quints and Mrs. Winkleman in the backyard, but also Jean.

"What's going on?" I asked, unlatching the gate and letting myself in. "How come you're home so early, Jean?"

"I managed to get my work finished, so I decided to come on home and get the kids settled down before the women came over."

"You knew about Michelle and Noel's moms?"

"Just this afternoon. Mrs. Lawrence got my work number from Mrs. Winkleman and called to see if it was really all right. I had to pretend I knew about it, but the whole thing was news to me." Jean separated Craig and Drew, who were fighting over the same ball. "Craig, here's one for you." She tossed it toward him and both boys went for it and started fighting again.

"I'm going in the house to change and get rid of my books," I said.

"Come back out, will you, Natalie? I don't know Mrs. Lawrence, and would hardly recognize Michelle's mother if I met her on the street. I'd like to have you around."

"Okay." I hesitated at the door, and then realized Jean must have turned off the alarm.

I had just gotten into my jeans and sweatshirt when the front doorbell rang. I dashed down and opened the door. There they all were: Mrs. Lawrence, Michelle's mother, Michelle, and Noel. "Hi," I said, going on out. "Everyone's in the backyard." I didn't want them in the house, because at this time of day it usually looked like a cyclone had struck.

"Sweetie, how are you?" Michelle's mom said to me as we started off. "I haven't seen you in ages." She was such a phony.

"I'm fine." Turning to Mrs. Lawrence, I said, "I didn't realize you wanted to meet the quints. You know, you could have come over any time."

"Oh, but I did not wish to intrude," she said in her French-accented voice. "It must be formidable . . . looking after so many little ones."

"Yes, at times." We were at the back now. "Well,

143

there they are!'' The quints all happened to be near the gate, as though they were expecting callers.

Mrs. Lawrence clasped her hands. ''Adorable! Simply adorable!''

In spite of myself, I felt a little flutter of pride.

''And this is Jean,'' I said. ''My . . . the quints' mother.''

They said hellos, and Jean opened the gate. ''Please come on in.''

Noel, the gentleman, introduced all the ladies, and then Jean named off the quints.

Mrs. Lawrence, wearing a tweed suit and loafers, stooped down and spoke to Alice, who was standing shyly, a finger in her mouth. Then Alice went forward and put that same finger on Mrs. Lawrence's cheek. The woman didn't seem to mind the wetness at all. With her hands around Alice, she looked up and said to Jean, ''She's just precious. They all are. What a lovely, lovely bunch of children.''

Michelle's mother, by contrast, steered clear of actual contact with the quints. In fact, when Drew came near and reached to touch her coat, she stepped back. She was perfectly groomed, as usual. I'd never ever seen her dressed the least bit casually, the way most mothers did around the house. She even wore total make-up at all times, and her hair always looked as though she'd just been to the beauty shop.

Mrs. Lawrence was deep into conversation with Jean and Mrs. Winkleman, and Noel and I were sprinting after Craig, who was headed for the open gate. Suddenly Michelle's mother gave a shout.

''For heaven's sakes!'' she yelled. ''Michelle, put it down!''

144

I looked around. The "it" was Emma, whom Michelle had picked up and was kissing on the cheek.

Startled, Michelle almost dropped the baby. She looked up guiltily as her mother stalked toward her. "I should think you'd know better," she said, putting her hand on Michelle's shoulder and ushering her away from the baby, now standing alone and bewildered. "You can't take any chances on picking up germs, not with that big photo session coming up."

I picked up Emma and Noel closed the gate.

Still with an anchor hold on Michelle, her mother rejoined the other women, who had stopped talking to take in the little scene.

"This little daughter of mine doesn't realize how delicate and susceptible she is. I've got to watch her every minute."

"Ummm." Noel's mother swept a glance over the woman, then picked up her conversation with Jean and the sitter.

Michelle, still under the hand of her mother, stared at the ground.

Noel went after a ball that had rolled to the fence. I followed. "How can your mother be friends with a woman like that?"

Noel bounced the ball to Beth. "They're not what you'd call real friends. It's just that we're new here and Mom doesn't know all that many people yet. But give her time."

I could understand that. And I also understood something else. Noel wasn't involved with Michelle as a *girl*. His feeling toward her seemed more like concern. And pity. I liked him even more, for caring about Michelle that way.

After they'd left, Jean chatted about Noel's mother . . . how warm and friendly she was, and "such a charming accent!"

"You'd barely met Michelle's mother before," I said. "Do you consider her warm and friendly, too?"

Jean eyed me. "No comment."

Mrs. Winkleman had an opinion, and stated it when we were in the house, unbundling the quints. "I don't know how that woman could say our babies have germs." She sniffed. "They're angels. Angels don't have germs."

Jean laughed. "I don't know about the angel part, but I can't believe these kids are a threat to anyone's health."

I reeled off the whole story to Choo Choo later, on the phone. "I'm feeling more and more sorry for Michelle. She's like a robot."

"Yeh, with her mom at the controls."

"Now I understand why Michelle never comes over. She might catch some bug that would make her miss out on a photo shoot."

"You're probably right. So what else is new? Has the creep called yet?"

"It's too early. Usually the phone rings at around seven or eight o'clock."

"Remember to do what I said," Choo Choo reminded me. "Call Trish by name. In fact, call her a name. I could supply you with several choice ones."

"How about, 'Trish, you demented sleaze, go stick your head in a fish tank'?"

"I like that," Choo Choo said. "Only make it 'a fish tank full of piranhas.' "

"Sounds good. I'll do it."

146

*   *   *

We didn't get a call that night or on the weekend.

The calls were the farthest thing from my mind, though, because on Saturday afternoon I had a date with Noel! Well, I guess you could call it a date because we went to the movies together.

It happened like this: He phoned that same Friday night and we kidded around as usual. Then suddenly he said, "Want to go to the flicks tomorrow?"

"Tomorrow?"

"In the afternoon."

"Uh . . . well . . . sure." I could actually feel my pulse throbbing.

"It's the one about the kid athlete who went down the tubes."

"Oh. Okay." What did I care what film it was? I'd have seen *Godzilla Goes to the Miss Universe Pageant* if Noel had asked.

"Good. Pick you up around two."

For a while I sat around in a daze. Then I told myself I was making a big deal out of simply going to the movies. I replied that going with Noel *was* a big deal. Even if I paid my own way, which I intended to do.

His dad drove us to the theater. Noel was going to buy my ticket, but I wouldn't let him. "Why should you, just because you're a guy?" I said. And besides, I thought, if it didn't cost too much, he might ask me to go again.

By the time we got out it was almost 6:00 P.M. "Do you have to get right home, or could we stop down the street for hamburgers?" Noel asked.

I told him I'd have to call, and did. It was okay.

147

Noel said one of his parents would pick us up when we'd finished.

Whenever the girls and I went to a movie together, we'd usually rip it apart afterward. Choo Choo was especially critical because she had an aunt who took part in community theater, and Choo Choo believed this connection made her some kind of expert on acting.

With Noel, it was different. He wanted to compare ideas with me about why the guy in the movie felt distanced from his classmates.

"Do you agree that he had no choice but to go with the tough crowd, then?" Noel wondered.

We argued a bit about the kid's options. I'm not saying it was a heavy conversation, because it wasn't. But I found I liked the idea of talking to a boy seriously, instead of just snapping out comments to make myself sound cute or witty.

I was curious, and not being known for my shyness, I just out and asked Noel if he had any friends who happened to be girls, from where he'd lived before.

"Sure," he said, dipping his French fry in vinegar (a custom they had in Canada, I learned). "Why not? Girls are people."

"Right. Do you miss them much? Your friends back there?"

"Now and then. But my family likes to travel, so I'll get up to Canada before long. Maybe for skiing, over the holidays. Do you ski?"

"Not really. I was going to learn, though; Jean and Dad were going to teach me. That was another plan that got scuttled by the quints."

"Where would you have gone?"

"Vail or Aspen, I guess. It's funny, my mother lives right in the middle of that territory, but she's not the least bit athletic."

"What's she like? I mean, what does your mother do, besides teach?"

"She likes music . . . *real* music, as she calls it. And ballet and theater, all that cultural stuff. She's sweet, and can be funny, in her own quiet way."

"You must miss her a lot."

"Yeh, I do. More, since I saw her last summer. Sometimes I see her face and hear her voice and . . ." I took a sip of Pepsi. "I'd rather not talk about it."

Noel didn't let the subject go, though. "If you miss her that much, how come you don't go out and live with her?"

I bit my lips to get control. I hadn't revealed this to anyone, but suddenly I thought I could, to Noel. "She begged me to stay when I was out there. Well, maybe *beg* is too strong a word. But she really wanted me to, a lot."

"And?"

I sniffed, and then struggled to smile. "I thought I'd miss everyone here too much. It seemed I just had to get back. But when I did, things weren't all that great. Everything revolves around the quints at home. It isn't anyone's fault, it's just the way things are. Even my friends seem a little different. I guess we're just not as close as we used to be, when we did everything together."

Noel shoved a slice of tomato back into the bun. "I thought I'd miss my friends a lot when we moved here. I do sometimes, but I'm gradually meeting new people. And then, as I said, my folks and I travel a lot, so it's not as though I'll be totally out of touch with the old gang."

We finished eating and walked outside to a phone booth. Noel called home, and his mother must have answered because he spoke French. I really marveled at the way he rattled it off.

"Wow," I said when he'd hung up. "I'll never learn to speak like that."

He smiled. "Hey, I made you my best offer. Hang around me. You'll pick it up in no time."

"How, when all you speak is English?"

He raised his eyebrows and rattled off a bunch of French I couldn't begin to understand.

"Give me a break," I said. "Start off with something simple."

"Okay. How's this? *Vous êtes ma chère amie.*"

"Same here." I was pretty sure he'd said I was his dear friend.

We walked over to the curb and waited for his mom. Noel looked at his watch. Then he draped an arm around my shoulder. "I'd miss you a lot if you decided to go live with your mother."

"You would?"

"Sure. You really are my best friend here."

I was dumbfounded. "I am?" My voice squeaked a little.

He laughed, withdrew his arm, and put his hands in his pockets. "Sure. I can talk to you. You have good sense and you're bright. And also quite wacky. I like that in a girl."

"I thought Michelle was your best friend."

"Michelle? You must be kidding."

"But . . ."

"Michelle's more like a relative . . . a cousin. I know her too well. I guess that's why I'm worried about the way she's been acting lately.

"I think she should go talk to Ms. Bredlow . . . the counselor."

"Huh. It's her mother that needs counseling. And speaking of mothers, here's mine."

Almost as though this was the day for mothers, Jean told me when I got home that mine had called.

"What did she want?"

"Just to talk, I guess." Jean was in her room, putting away clothes from the cleaners.

"Did you tell I was out with a boy?"

"Hey, give me credit." Jean removed a plastic cover and knotted it. She always did that, to keep a baby from getting caught in it and maybe suffocating. "How *was* your date, by the way?"

"Noel told me I was his best friend." When Jean gave me a look, I said, "Is that bad?"

"Actually," she said, "I think that's great. You should consider it a compliment."

"Why do you say that?"

Jean closed the closet door. "It means he really likes *you*. You know, sweetie, boyfriends don't necessarily last, but a boy who's a friend can be a friend forever."

"I never thought of that."

She put an arm around me as we walked out of the room. "Natalie, you have no cause for worry. You'll always have friends. You're that kind of person."

I didn't wonder too much about what Mother was

calling about. She checked me out most weekends. The conversation usually had a lot to do with school-work and how I was keeping up. And it usually also had something to do with why I hadn't written, so I was more or less prepared.

Only this time our conversation was different.

After a bit about this and that, Mother suddenly said, "Natalie, is it okay if this time I'm the one who changes her mind?"

"About what?"

She hesitated. "Darling, ever since you called about coming out I've been in a constant state of . . . I don't know. Guilt, longing. I felt so bad afterward, I still do, that when you reached out to me, I . . . I . . ." Her voice was trembling. I waited, not knowing what to say.

"Natalie, I do want you to come out. Now. Soon. Whenever you feel that you could. I miss you like . . . I don't know. Nothing that I'm doing is nearly so important as having you with me. Can you believe that?"

"Well . . ." I felt all mixed-up.

"The classes can go. All the extra things can be canceled if they have to be. Nothing really matters so much as our being together."

I took a deep breath. This was too sudden.

"Natalie? . . . What do you think?" She paused. "Or have you changed your mind again?" Then quickly she added, "I didn't mean that as a rebuke. It's only natural that you should have, after . . ."

I finally found my voice. "It isn't that I've changed my mind, Mother. It's just that—"

"I know. That I caught you off guard."

"Yes, that's it."

"I don't want to rush you, sweetheart. Think about it. If you feel you can't make the change right now, I'll understand. But do think about it, will you?"

"Yes, I will. Maybe later?"

"Of course. Well, that's what I called about. I've been in such a state lately, wondering, worrying . . ."

"There's nothing to worry about, Mother. I'm fine. But of course, I do miss you . . . and . . ."

"I know. Well, good-bye for now. Have a pleasant weekend, what's left of it, and think of me."

"Oh, I do. Every time I put a tape into the player you sent . . ."

"Oh, dear." She laughed. "I have a feeling I may regret that gift."

"No, you won't. I'll use the headphones when I'm there."

"That's a promise. 'Bye for now, sweet."

" 'Bye, Mother." After we'd hung up, I sat on the edge of the bed. I felt heavy, weighted down. Why did it always have to be like this? When I'd begged to go out, Mother had said, *Not now. Later, maybe*. And now she was saying, *Forget all that. Come out right away*. But now I wasn't sure I wanted to.

Why should I leave, when things were suddenly going right for me? Noel had turned into a really good friend . . . more, maybe. And at school I was suddenly someone. It sounded shallow, but doesn't everyone want to be special in some way? Well, now I was.

So what could I tell Mother? I mean, without hurting her feelings? I didn't know.

Sighing, I got up. I didn't have to decide right away. Maybe something would happen. Something that would help me explain why I had to stay around here. Something Mother could accept. It seemed entirely possible. So much had been going on lately that I wouldn't be surprised at anything. Anything at all.

That's what I thought that afternoon. Boy, was I wrong!

18

○■○■○

I was a little later than usual getting to school Monday morning. The halls were deserted, except for some girls, part of Trish's fan club, that rounded the hall and nearly bumped into me. They didn't even notice. They were laughing among themselves.

I'd just got my books for morning classes out of my locker when I noticed Michelle standing down the hall a little way, facing away from me. Her head was bent and she seemed almost to be cringing.

"Michelle?" I walked toward her. "Michelle, is something wrong?"

She turned and looked at me. I almost fainted. The make-up was not to be believed! Base, rouge, and eye-stuff going all the way to her eyebrows in various shades of lavender and gray. The eyebrows had been plucked to a thin line, and her hair, I now saw, was pulled into a stiff, sophisticated "do" and lacquered.

"Michelle . . . why . . . ?" I didn't know what to say.

"You think I look awful," she said in a whispery voice.

"No, I don't think . . ." Actually, she looked worse than awful. Grotesque. Fakey. Like a mask of someone else. "Uh . . . why . . . ?"

"I have to go for test shots after school," she mumbled, head down.

"Test shots for what?"

"Evening gowns."

"Evening gowns!"

"I'm too old for teens. Besides, my sister Nicole—"

"Michelle, you *are* a teen." And just barely, at that.

"But models always have to look older."

"Says who?"

"My mother." Michelle ran her hands down her sides. "I think I look funny, wearing these clothes . . ."

I wanted to say it wasn't the jeans that were out of place, but her face. She felt so bad, though, I lied and told her everyone would understand. "After all, you can't wear an evening gown to school," I said, trying to console her. "Everyone will realize that." *Sure, they will,* I thought.

I walked close to her, down the hall. I hated to leave her to face the stares alone in her homeroom, but there was nothing I could do.

She didn't show up for lunch.

"Have you seen Michelle?" I asked the girls.

"Oh, have I ever!" Choo Choo said. "Bride of Frankenstein."

"Her mother made her wear that stuff," I said.

"What stuff?" Jiggs asked, ripping open a bag of potato chips.

"Just ten tons of make-up," Choo Choo said. "All the kids are talking about it. Especially you-know-who."

"Oh, oh, oh!" Jiggs yelped. "Speaking of Trish-the-fish, I have a news flash. Guess what!"

"I can't imagine," Choo Choo said.

"This is the absolute truth. I got it directly from Troy. Guess what he told me!"

"Oh, spit it out," Choo Choo said. "For heaven's sakes."

"Trish told Troy, and Troy told me, that *she* has been making phone calls to your house, Natalie. *The* calls!"

"You're kidding!" I gasped. "I mean, did she really do it?"

"If you remember, I told you all along it was Trish," Choo Choo said.

"I don't get it," I said. "If she did do it, why would she tell Troy?"

"Because she actually thought it was funny, and clever, I guess," Jiggs said. "And she thought he'd get a big charge out of it. Only he didn't."

"So why did Troy tell *you?*" Claudia asked Jiggs. "And not Natalie?"

"Because he thinks Natalie doesn't like him. And he felt shy." Jiggs gave an elaborate shrug. "Don't ask me why. That's what he said. And that's what I'm telling you."

"That Trish is just so immature," Choo Choo said. "She shouldn't be allowed to wander around without her nanny."

157

"Immature isn't the word," I said. *"Mean, vindictive,* they're more like it. When I think of what she put us all through! Especially Jean. Jean's a nervous wreck." I looked over to the table where Trish was yakking it up with her crowd. "I'd like to go over there and punch her out!"

"Hey, I'm for that!" Jiggs said. "We could pulverize the whole bunch, even if they do outnumber us. Shall we do it?"

I backed down. "I don't want to make a scene. Anyway, why give her the satisfaction of knowing she upset us so at home. She'd probably hate it more just to be ignored."

"Oh, Natalie, you're so right about that," Choo Choo said. "Dear Trish does like being the center of attention." She picked up her tray and Jiggs and I followed. "Speaking of attention, where do you suppose Michelle is hiding out . . . so as not to get any? Attention."

And then we said it together—"The washroom!"

We took off for the washroom, but Michelle wasn't there.

I didn't see her the rest of the afternoon. I assumed, after a while, that she'd just gone home. Who could blame her? Poor Michelle.

After my last class I ran into Ms. Bredlow, who chatted with me about the quints' birthday. That made me late leaving the school, so I didn't see Noel as I walked home—but I could almost imagine him with me. Once again, for about the trillionth time, I replayed what he'd said about my being his best friend. And I could almost feel his arm around me again, even though it had been for only a few moments.

Noel was so different from most boys, who were constantly showing off. Especially Troy. Even if Troy did call and tell me about Trish, it wouldn't make any difference. I'd never like him again.

I wondered what Dad would do when he found out who had made those calls. Would he ream Trish out, call her parents? I'd rather avoid all that by not telling, but I had to do it. Just to calm Jean down, if for no other reason.

I was a few doors from home when I heard a car tearing down the street. It sped past me, and then brakes squealed loudly. Jean! She careened into our driveway, and almost before the car stopped she was out of it and running into the house. I started running, too. What could be wrong? Had she heard about Trish? What was she going to do?

The front door was partly open. As I raced in, I heard Mrs. Winkleman crying hysterically, and Jean shouting.

"How could this happen?" I heard her yelling. "How long ago?" I could also hear the quints screaming.

I rushed to the kitchen, and they all seemed to be there. "What's wrong?" I shouted above the noise.

Jean, looking frenzied, said, "Alice is missing!"

"Alice?" I looked around. Sure enough, there were only four quints. "Where is she?" was what I said, even though it made no sense.

"That's what we don't know!" Jean shouted, and then to Mrs. Winkleman, "How long were you in the house? How long on the telephone?"

"Not long. Not long at all." The sitter's hands were clenched against her chest, almost as though in prayer.

"This woman called and started telling me about a nursery school and I said she should call back later when you were home and . . ." She began to sob harder than ever. "I was only in the house for a few minutes. That's the truth. And when I went back outside, she was gone . . . our little Alice!"

I knelt and pulled the crying children close to me. They were still in outdoors clothes.

"And you're sure the gate to the fence was fastened?" Jean asked, not shouting now, but still agitated. "Alice couldn't have wandered out?"

"I know it was fastened! I know it was! Oh, who could have done this brutal thing? The poor baby!"

"I'm calling the police," Jean said. "Or Jack. Both."

"I'll go out and look again," Mrs. Winkleman said, blowing her nose. "Maybe she's hiding." She hurried out the door.

"Jean," I said, "don't call the police yet. Maybe Mrs. Winkleman just *thinks* she fastened the gate. Let's look around the neighborhood."

"It's no use. They've taken her, I know. Remember that last call? 'This is the final warning!' " Jean was getting hysterical again. "My baby has been kidnapped, and I'm calling the police!"

"Jean, a girl at school, Trish, made those calls. I just found out today."

"Then she's the one!" Jean grabbed the phone. "If she's mean enough to make calls, she's mean enough to take Alice! What's her number?"

I told her, and then herded the quints to their room. Only without Alice, they weren't quints anymore. I felt weak. Could Trish really have taken her, our baby?

I couldn't believe she'd go that far. Trish was rotten in many ways, but didn't she know about kidnapping? It was a federal offense, not just a kid prank.

Without bothering to change their clothes, I spent a few minutes getting the four babies interested in toys, and then, after closing the gate to their room, I hurried back toward the kitchen. I could hear a male voice, only it wasn't Dad's.

"Noel!" I was so surprised to see him. "How did you hear about it so fast?"

"I didn't. I just came over to see if Michelle was hiding out here. Her mother's going crazy. She went to the school to pick up Michelle, but she's vanished." He looked first at Jean, who was almost hyperventilating, and then at me. "Now I hear one of the quints is missing."

"Yes . . . Alice. My sister! My sister is gone!"

"Kidnapped," Jean said. "I know it. That Trish girl wasn't home. She's taken Alice all right."

To Noel, who now seemed totally confused, I said, "Choo Choo found out it was Trish who made those threatening calls." I wasn't sure whether I'd even told him about them. And then to Jean, I said, "I guess maybe you *should* call the police. And Dad."

"I just did." She dropped onto a chair, and bending her head on her arms, started sobbing. "My baby . . . my baby."

Mrs. Winkleman came in, looking more frightened than before. "There's not a sign of her out back."

I took the woman's arm and steered her toward the hall. "Why don't you go in and quiet the other four?" They were crying again.

Sobbing even harder, the sitter went to them.

161

Now, looking alarmed himself, Noel said, "I'll scout around the neighborhood, just in case." And left.

"Jean, we'll get her back," I said, leaning down and smoothing her hair. "Trish wouldn't hurt Alice. She's just trying to scare us."

"Why would she do that?" Jean's voice was muffled.

"Because she hates me."

"But to take a baby, a little innocent baby!"

"I know." To myself, I was saying, *I hope it was Trish . . . better Trish than a real . . .* oh, but I didn't want to think of that possibility. There wasn't anything to do but wait for the police. I just kept on trying to reassure Jean.

"Natalie . . ."

I looked up. Noel, with a very strange expression on his face, was standing by the back door. "You want to come out here? I've something to show you." And when Jean lifted her head, Noel beckoned. "Come along, both of you."

I can't describe how I felt at that moment. All the horror stories I'd ever heard rushed into my mind. And Noel, looking white-faced, wasn't saying what he found. *Not the body!* I whispered to myself. *Not the body!*

"You've found her." Jean sounded both hopeful and panicked. "Is she . . . oh, is she . . ."

"She's okay," Noel said. "Come along, I'll show you."

We went outside and through the gate to the driveway. Then we followed Noel along the side of the house to the front, and then toward the other side. Noel was walking fast, and Jean and I followed, clinging together. When we rounded the corner, Noel stopped and put his finger to his lips. He pointed.

Jean and I rushed forward, and then we stopped abruptly. I couldn't believe what I was seeing. Michelle was crouched against the house, next to some big bushes . . . and she was holding Alice!

We froze. Then, with a cry, Jean dashed toward them, and scooped up the sleeping baby. Jean was making strange, animal sounds, and Alice, lifting her head, began crying.

"Shhh, be quiet, you'll frighten her," Michelle said, still crouched. "You're making her cry. Don't let her cry."

"Michelle," Noel said, "What on earth . . ."

Michelle looked toward him. Her face was streaked with rivulets of color from her weird eye make-up. "Oh, hi Noel," she said in an ordinary voice. "What are you doing here?"

"Michelle, how could you do this?" I gasped. "How could you take Alice and . . ."

Then in a strange kind of tone, Michelle said, "You mean *this* Lovey-Baby? I just wanted to hold her."

Noel gave me a puzzled look.

"Lovey-Baby is her doll," I explained.

And now Jean came back to reality. "You—you monster!" she shouted at the huddled girl. "How could you do this to us?"

"I didn't hurt her. I didn't make her cry." Michelle got up. "It's only one baby, you know. I only borrowed one of them. You have all those others." She reached out to touch Alice's foot, but Jean stepped back.

"You think that makes a difference?" Jean stared

hard at Michelle. "She's my baby. No matter how many children a mother has, she loves and cherishes every one of them!"

Michelle wrinkled her forehead, as though trying to understand. "She does?"

"Oh, Michelle." I put my arms around her now trembling shoulders. I just couldn't help feeling sorry for her, she looked so alone and unhappy and confused.

Noel put his arms around both of us and then said, "Michelle, let's go to my house now. Okay? I'll look after you."

"All right."

Noel, with his arm just around Michelle now, said to Jean, "Is it okay, Mrs. Wentworth? Is it all right if she goes with me?"

Jean nodded. "It's okay."

We all walked to the front of the house, and then Noel, talking in low tones to her, guided Michelle down the street.

I was glad they left when they did, because just then a police car rolled up. Jean and I waited until the two patrolmen walked over to us.

I was hoping Jean wouldn't tell them about Michelle, but I guess she had to. She tried to tone it down, though, by saying the girl had just come over to play with the children, and had taken one of them outside the yard.

The police said they had to make a report anyway, so they came into the house. Mrs. Winkleman started sobbing again when she saw Alice, and reached out for her, but Alice clung to her mother.

The sitter described to the police how she had heard

the phone ringing when they were all outdoors, and how she'd come in, talked a few minutes, and then, going outside again, discovered one baby missing. "So then I called Mrs. Wentworth, and kept praying. And the Lord heard my prayers," she said. The police didn't write that part down.

"Now, what about this girl?" the officer with the pad wanted to know. "Who is she and why was she here?"

I broke in to say she was a friend of mine, and then had to explain who I was, and my age, and all that stuff. Then I told them Michelle had just borrowed Alice. "She didn't know we'd be worried." That was true. Michelle had seemed quite surprised by the way Jean and I had carried on. There was something really wrong with her, I knew that now.

The officers left just before Dad slammed into the house. When he saw Alice he stopped short. "You found her! Where was she?"

We went through the story, Jean and I, and then we all walked back to the nursery. Mrs. Winkleman looked apprehensive when she saw Dad.

He didn't blow up, though. Maybe it was because he'd arrived after it was all over. The sitter explained again about the call, and this time she was calm enough to say it was our former sitter, Mrs. Hinley, who'd called. It seemed her daughter-in-law was starting a pre-nursery school and wondered if the folks would be interested in enrolling the quints.

"No way!" Jean said. "I'll never leave them out of my sight again!" (The next day, when she was herself again, Jean called Mrs. Hinley and said she'd consider

165

sending the babies when they were a few months older.)

When Dad said he was going to Noel's to "see about that girl," I said I wanted to go along.

As we started down the street, I looked up at Dad. He was like a dragon, breathing smoke and fire. I put my hand on his arm and he stopped. "What? What is it?"

"Dad, don't yell at Michelle, okay?"

"Don't yell at a girl who took your baby sister and scared us half to death? What's wrong with you, Natalie?"

"Dad, it's what's wrong with *Michelle*. She's sick, I know it. Otherwise, she'd never do a thing like that."

"Huh." He started walking again. "She'll be even sicker when I get through with her!"

"Oh, Dad." I trembled for poor Michelle, but what could I do? When my father gets riled up, there's no reasoning with him.

Noel met us at the door. "Where is she?" was all my Dad said.

Before Noel could answer, his mother and Michelle's mom, too, walked over to Dad and they all started talking.

I didn't listen to what they were saying because I had spied Michelle, huddled at the end of the sofa. She looked like a rag doll left out in the rain, all limp, its face streaked with color.

"Oh, Michelle . . ." I went over, sat down, and reached toward her. With a frightened look, she cringed and moved even farther away.

Dad was still talking rather heatedly, but gradually he quieted down.

After a bit I heard Mrs. Lawrence say, in her softly accented voice, "I know it must have been a most terrible experience for you, Mr. Wentworth, but if you could find it in your heart . . ."

And then Michelle's mother, nervously twisting her rings, was assuring Dad that she would get help for Michelle. At that, Dad turned, and for the first time saw Michelle herself. The rest of his anger faded as his look turned to shock.

"Michelle? . . ." He seemed hardly able to recognize the girl he'd once thought so pretty. "Good heavens," he said softly, "what's happened to you?" And then he turned to her mother. "What have you done to your daughter? How could you let this happen?"

Hearing that, Michelle's mom started weeping so hard that Noel had to lead her from the room.

Poor Mrs. Lawrence, who was in the middle of all this, murmured that she was certain that Michelle and her whole family would seek help. "Things will be much better, you will see."

"All right." Dad seemed about to go to Michelle, but seeing her look of terror, he changed his mind and nodded to me. "Let's go, Natalie," he said. "Jean needs us." At the door, though, he couldn't resist saying to Noel's mother, "See that the girl gets that gook off her face, will you? That's the first thing."

"I will see to it." And then, almost shyly, she said, "Mr. Wentworth, I hope when we all meet again it will be, how do you say it? Under happier circumstances."

"I hope so."

She touched my shoulder. "Of course, I know your

167

delightful daughter Natalie, and I have also had the pleasure of meeting your wife and adorable young children.''

Not to be outdone by this politeness, Dad said, "And I hope to meet your husband. Your son Noel, he's a fine boy. Very fine. He and my little Natalie are good friends.''

When we left and were walking down the sidewalk, I said, "Dad, did you really have to say that?''

"Say what?''

"You called me *little Natalie!*''

"So?'' He put his arm around me and gave me a quick squeeze. "You *are* my little girl. That'll never change.''

"Okay.'' I had to give in. Dad would never change, either. At least not very much.

When we got back home, Mrs. Winkleman had gone and the quints were in their high chairs, eating animal crackers. Jean was standing by the phone. "How did it go?'' she asked, searching Dad's face. I knew she was wondering if he'd made a big scene.

"I told them what was what,'' he said, hanging up his jacket. "I didn't mince any words.''

Jean shot a quick look at me. I smiled and shrugged. She relaxed. "I know you did, honey,'' she said to Dad. "I'm sure you set them straight.'' Her face softened. "What about Michelle? Now that it's all over, I feel sorry for her. Poor little thing.'' And then, "I have a feeling she doesn't get much love. She has nothing to hang on to.''

"Her mother even got rid of Lovey-Baby,'' I said, and then explained, "That's a big doll she used to hold

168

all the time. Her mother threw it out. Now she doesn't have anything. I guess when she took Alice she just wanted something warm and cuddly to hold.''

Dad poured himself a cup of coffee. ''The shrink will have to deal with that. Jeanie, were you about to call someone?''

''My mother.''

''Your mother? How come? It isn't Saturday.'' He put a hand on her shoulder. ''You think you should tell her about Alice?''

''I don't know. All I do know is I need to talk to her.''

Dad leaned down and kissed her forehead. Then, still holding his coffee, he motioned for me to leave the room with him.

Out by the stairs I picked up my books from where I'd flung them . . . it seemed like hours ago. ''Dad,'' I said, ''you know what Michelle said to Jean? She said she didn't think it would matter if she took one of the babies, because we had so many.''

''Incredible.'' He picked up a notebook and handed it to me. ''As though that made a difference.''

''I know.'' I started up the stairs and then turned. ''Dad, what if you had only one . . . one child?''

''What do you mean?''

''If you had just . . . like one daughter? And then you didn't have her around anymore?''

''I don't want to think about it.'' He went into their bedroom and I proceeded upstairs.

In my room, I couldn't settle down. I felt all mixed-up inside. I'd hoped to find a good excuse to stay. But instead . . .

I suddenly felt drawn toward my mother's picture,

169

so familiar I'd stopped noticing it. But now I drifted over, picked it up, and really looked at it.

That half-smile was for whoever it was who took the photo. But the look in her eyes seemed almost meant for me, here and now. *Natalie,* she seemed to be saying, *don't you realize? Don't you understand?*

And as I stood, caught and held by my mother's gaze, I guess I did, for the very first time.

A mother needs her child. That had been shown to me so clearly today, by the panic and then relief on Jean's face. It had made no difference to her that there were other children. Jean needed this particular child. She needed Alice.

And here I was, my mother's only child, not lost, it's true, but out of reach. And when she'd called for me to come to her, I'd answered, "I'm not sure."

"Oh, Mom," I said to the photograph, "why didn't you let me know? Why didn't you coax?"

But that just wasn't her way. She'd never coax, or force, or play on sympathy. She wanted me willingly, or not at all.

I knew this now, and something else besides. I needed my mother just as much as she needed me.

19

───○■○■○───

I decided not to say anything right away. There had been so much excitement, I felt we all needed to calm down for a while. Also, I wanted to be sure, absolutely sure this time. Once I'd told everyone, there'd be no turning back. Not unless I wanted to look like a mindless ninny.

But more and more each day, I knew it was the right decision. It was going to happen. The only thing I wasn't sure about was *when*.

A strange thing took place. Now that I knew I was going to leave them, the quints didn't bug me the way they used to. I could look at them as if from a distance and relate to them not as pests but as little people who'd have problems of their own. Would they ever!

One night I said to Dad, "I think we should stop calling the babies 'the quints.' "

"Oh? What should we call them then?" He turned on the TV. His pilot show was about to begin.

"They have names, you know. What's wrong with calling them Alice, Beth and so on?"

Dad made a half-smile. "Here Comet, here Cupid, here Donder and Blitzen. And the next one. That takes a lot of time."

"But it's important, Dad. They need to be individuals."

"I'll try to keep that in mind."

"Dad, I'm serious!"

"Okay, okay, I'll take note." The show started. "Want to watch?"

As usual I didn't, but I sat down anyway.

Dad flung an arm around my shoulders. I'd miss moments like this. But I'd have them again, when I was here on visits, wouldn't I? Dad wasn't the 'keep in touch' type. It would be up to me to call in between visits. I promised myself that I'd do it. I'd try to be his Sparkles the way I used to be.

My eyes were focused on the planes swooping all over the screen, but my mind was centered on the . . . on Alice, Beth, Craig, Drew and Emma. I could see them in school. What a bummer it would be if all the kids, and the teachers, too, lumped them into one big glob of kids. I hated being called "the sister of the quints." But what about the quints themselves? How could they break away and simply be themselves?

"Dad," I said, when the commercials came on, "do you suppose the quints . . . I mean, well, you know who, could go to different schools?"

"Schools? You mean like first grade?"

"Yeh."

He sighed. "One step at a time, Natalie. They're not even into nursery school yet."

"I know. Isn't it great, though, about that woman starting one up? She's experienced, too."

172

"It'll be a break for Jeanie. For all of us." He kicked up the sound again. I'd been about to blurt out that I wouldn't be here, but I decided it could wait. I dreaded telling Dad more than anything.

A day or so later I happened to be at my locker when Noel came along. "How're you doing?" he said, pausing.

"Okay. Have you heard from Michelle?" She hadn't been at school since the incident.

"No, but her mother called mine and said Michelle was 'resting up' somewhere. I'm sure she'll be all right." He gave me a big smile. "What's new in your life?"

Suddenly I wanted to tell Noel about my decision. Maybe to check it out. "Could I talk to you . . . about something?"

"Sure." He eyed me. "When?"

"Maybe after school? Or do you have a rehearsal?"

"Not tonight. I'll meet you out front."

It was really nice, I thought, the way he didn't pressure me to tell him right away.

When we were walking home, Noel still didn't ask, but let me find the right moment.

"It's about my mother," I finally said. "Remember I told you how she wants me to move out there? To Colorado?"

"Yeh. So you've decided to do it."

I stopped. "How did you know?"

Stopping, too, he smiled and said, "You've been on the verge of doing it a long time, I could tell."

"Noel, how could you tell, if I couldn't?"

He laughed, took my arm, and we started walking

173

again. "You couldn't see your face when you talked about your mother. I could. It was pretty clear to me you'd go eventually." After a pause, he said, "I hope it's not right away, though."

"Why?" *Tell me it would break your heart, Noel!*

"Because you've got to see me through this play. You're my advisor, my coach, maybe my whole fan club."

"You ham. You'll do fine. But I won't go right away. Probably not until the semester break. I want to wind up my classes and everything."

"And," Noel reminded me, "you've got to get some of that *parlez-vous* stuff under your belt . . . show your mom you can do it." He paused. "It may mean we'll have to spend a lot of time together, but I'm willing to make the sacrifice, if you are."

"Yeh, I guess you're right," I agreed. "We'll just have to tough it out."

We shifted to other subjects then, but underneath the talk I was thinking, *Noel and I will stay good friends. I'll see him a lot, and who knows? In time we may become more than friends.*

I really hadn't intended to tell Choo Choo and Jiggs before telling my own family, but it just came out the next day when we were finishing up lunch.

Trish was walking by with her empty tray when Jiggs said loudly, "Is it true, Natalie, that the FBI traced those calls to your house and are about to move in for an arrest?"

Trish dropped the tray and rushed out the door.

"Jiggs," I said, laughing, "that was mean."

"No, it wasn't," Choo Choo said, digging a mirror

out of her purse. She checked her lipstick. "Trish deserves worse than that. Let's think of ways to make her life miserable the whole rest of the school year, right up to graduation."

"I won't be here that long," I blurted out, unthinking.

Both girls stared at me. Choo Choo shoved the mirror back into her purse. "Oh, don't tell me, Natalie! You have something fatal, some dread disease. Oh . . . and so brave . . ."

"Knock it off, Claudia," I said. "What I meant is I'm moving out to my mother's."

"Your mother's!"

The girls started bombarding me with questions, and I kept assuring them I'd still be here for the really big events like the play and a basketball playoff. I'd be back for summers and vacations, too. And then we talked about their coming out to visit me, and the fun we'd have.

"What do your folks, I mean Jean and your father, think about this move?" Choo Choo asked as we got up and cleared the table. "I'll bet they're all broken up."

"Actually, they don't know. I haven't told them yet." I was wishing I hadn't told the girls, either, especially when Choo Choo came up with a suggestion.

"I know how hard it must be for you," she said, looking like a tragic heroine from some old-time movie. "Would you like me to break the news for you, Natalie? Gently?"

I panicked. "No! Don't say a word! I've got to do it myself."

And I knew I'd better do it soon. I just didn't trust Choo Choo to keep this to herself—not with her flair for the dramatic.

When I got home from school, I joined Jean in the nursery. As usual, I had to give the quints horsey rides.

Jean looked on, smiling. "Your father told me what you said about calling them 'the quints,' and I absolutely agree. We've got to think of ways of separating them now and then, too. Let each one be 'the baby' instead of a package deal. Beth," she took that baby in her arms. "Your name is Beth Wentworth. You got that?"

"Yeh, Bethie," I chimed in. "And if anyone calls you 'quint' just punch their ticket."

Jean laughed. "I have a feeling they'll all be fighters, from the looks of them. Oh, hey," she pulled Craig and Drew apart. "You don't have to take me literally. Now, stop hitting!"

"Would you let one or two come out to visit me? Like, they could take turns?"

"What?"

And then I realized what I'd said. "Jean . . ." I looked at her and then away. "I have to tell you something."

"Oh, no." Her eyes widened and she stared at me.

"I've decided to go live with my mother." I bent my head to keep from seeing her expression.

"I guess . . ." her voice cracked. "I knew it. I could feel it coming on."

"How did you know?" I thought I'd been so cool.

"It's hard to say. I just sensed you were missing

your mom more and more." She hugged Emma and kissed the top of her head. "I understand, Natalie. And I'm glad for you. And your mother. But . . ." her eyes misted over. "But I'm going to miss you like crazy. You're like . . . I don't know. A friend. A little sister."

"Oh, Jean." I wrapped my arms around her and around the baby. "Now that it's settled in my mind, I've started feeling like the big sister of these guys. You know, close. Do you really think I could take one now and then . . . to my Mom's?"

"Honey, I don't know how she'd feel about that. But you'll come here, won't you? Whenever you can?"

"How about all summer? Or most of it? And holidays?"

"That would be wonderful!"

"And I'll call my sisters and brothers, too . . . if they ever learn to say more than 'Lee, Lee,' or ' 'Sey, 'sey' for *horsey*."

"No!" Craig pulled a toy elephant from Alice. "Mine!"

"Just listen to that!" Jean said. "They're learning more every day!"

When I went upstairs, I took Emma with me. The littlest. The sweetest. I'd miss her most of all.

I sat her on the bed and kneeled beside it. "Emma, I have to tell you something," I said. She put her finger in her mouth and looked solemnly at me. "Natalie is going to go bye-bye soon. Far away. She's going to go live with her mommy."

Emma took her finger out of her mouth. "Mom-ee," she said.

"That's right. But I'll always be your big sister. I want you to remember that. And I'll come home and be with you . . . lots of times. And I'll think of you, and tell my new friends about you. But you know what I'll call you?"

She put her head forward, and we pressed foreheads together. "I'll call you my sister, Emma. And I want you to remember that, Emma. You have a name, and don't you let any kids get off calling you 'quint.' You understand?"

"I do."

I looked around, startled. Dad was standing in the doorway.

"I'll remember that," he said.

Our eyes met. I could tell he knew.

He came toward me and I stood and threw my arms around him. I was crying, and I guess he was, too. "Oh, babe, are you really going to leave us?"

"Not for all the time. Just—"

"Has it really been so bad for you here?" His voice was so choked he could hardly get out the words. "I know we've taken terrible advantage of you, but—"

"No, you haven't."

"But I didn't realize . . ." He paused. "What made you decide to do this? To leave us?"

How could I answer that? I didn't know, exactly. "Well . . . when Alice was missing . . ."

"Yes? . . ."

"The look on Jean's face, the, I don't know, the pain . . ."

"Go on." He wasn't making it easy for me.

"I guess it made me realize how awful it could be . . . to lose a child."

Dad held me tight. "But no one stole you from your mother."

"I know, but . . ." I pulled away slightly and looked at him. "Oh, can't you see? Mother needs me. She really does."

"Don't you think we need you, too? Don't you think we love you just as much?"

"Yes, but . . . I'm all she has." I could feel the tears starting again.

"Honey, she wouldn't want you to come there out of pity. Your mother isn't that way."

"Dad, it's not pity. I want my mother! I want to be with her!" The tears came pouring out then.

Smoothing my hair, he said, "I know, Sparkles, I know." He sounded so sad. "I can understand. But don't forget, we want you, too. You'll come out often, won't you? To see us?"

"I promise. I'll wear out the suitcase you gave me."

He held me close. "You're still my little girl, my firstborn, and you always will be."

"I know, Dad. I really do."

After Dad left, I lay on my bed and cried and cried. Oh, why did it have to be so hard . . . why did I have to make a choice? I thought of all the people I'd leave behind—my family, my friends, my—Noel. Did I really want to give them up to be with my mother?

I did. I knew I did. The feeling for her was so strong that I knew it couldn't be any other way. Why had it taken me so long to figure that out?

There was one more thing I needed to do. Call Mother. Would she still want me? Or would she be sorry she'd asked me to come to Colorado?

I needn't have worried.

At first, when I told her, Mother gave a gasp of joy. And then she said, "Oh, Natalie, are you sure? Are you really sure?"

"Mother, this time I'm absolutely certain. I've changed my mind for the very last time." And then I added, "So don't go out and buy any bubble gum."

"Darling, you can change your mind about other things if you must. But please, not about this." She hesitated and then said shakily, "You can't imagine how I've been hoping . . . dreaming you'd make this call."

I felt all other thoughts wash away. Nothing else mattered. Just this.

"Mother? . . ."

"Yes?"

"Just . . ." I couldn't say it right now. It wasn't quite clear. "Would it be okay if I called you later? Right now I—"

"I understand. I feel the same way. Until later then, Natalie."

I sat there for a while, staring at the phone, wondering what it was . . . that thought I couldn't express. And then it came to me.

I was finally going home. Not running *from* home, but running *to* it.

And this time out of love.

About the Author

STELLA PEVSNER was born in Lincoln, Illinois, and attended Illinois State University and studied advertising at Northwestern. She and her husband live in a suburb of Chicago with a multitude of cats. They have four grown children, all confirmed animal lovers. Ms. Pevsner is the author of *AND YOU GIVE ME A PAIN, ELAINE* and *CUTE IS A FOUR-LETTER WORD*, available from Archway Paperbacks, and the Minstrel Book *ME, MY GOAT, AND MY SISTER'S WEDDING*.